The Ritual of Pearls

New *X Rated* titles from *X Libris*:

Other titles in the *X Libris* series:

The Ritual of Pearls

Susan Swann

LIBRIS

An *X Libris* Book

First published by X Libris in 1995
Reprinted 1999, 2001

Copyright © Susan Swann 1995

A CIP catalogue for this book
is available from the British Library.

ISBN 0 7515 1570 1

Photoset in North Wales by
Derek Doyle & Associates, Mold, Clwyd
Printed and bound in Great Britain by
Clays Ltd, St Ives plc

X Libris
A Division of
Little, Brown and Company (UK)
Brettenham House
Lancaster Place
London WC2E 7EN

www.xratedbooks.co.uk

The Ritual of Pearls

Chapter One

MARIKA FREMEN UNCROSSED her slim legs and rose to her feet. She began stacking papers into her black briefcase.

'Thank you for your time, Mr Danvers. I'm glad everything met with your approval. I'll be in touch again soon.' Her voice was low-pitched, professional.

'A pleasure to work with you, Miss Fremen,' Danvers said smoothly. 'I look forward to seeing how your proposals come together.'

He was the owner of a firm which produced exclusive but traditional silk lingerie, with major outlets all over England. By employing a talented new designer and seeking the advice of Marika's prestigious PR company, he was hoping to give his products a more upmarket image. A small, stocky man in his late fifties, he wore an expensive, well-cut suit which still did nothing to disguise his paunch. Although his expression was mild his eyes were predatory.

Reaching into the drawer of his black ash and chrome desk, Danvers drew out a slim white box bearing the new company logo. Sliding it towards Marika, he said, 'I hope you'll accept this with my compliments. It's one of our newest designs. I'm sure it will fit.' His eyes moved slowly over the contours of her cream wool jacket. 'Thirty-six "C" cup, twenty-four waist, thirty-six hip? Correct me if I'm mistaken.'

Marika didn't answer. She threw him a tight smile as she picked up the box and thanked him coolly for the gift.

'I knew I was right about the size,' Danvers said with satisfaction. 'Assessing the needs of beautiful women is part of my profession. You know, if you ever get sick of working for PrimeLight, you could come and work for me. I'd pay you well. Have you ever considered going into modelling? Lingerie looks best on a tall, curvy woman. You've got the figure for it – and the looks.'

You couldn't afford me, she thought, but she said, 'I don't think so. I like working in PR and I'm good at it. But I think you know that. Otherwise I wouldn't be here.'

'Ouch. A modern woman through and through, eh? Emmeline Pankhurst had a lot to answer for. Pity. I was going to ask you out to dinner.'

No doubt he had her tagged as a hard-nosed career woman who had no time for men or sex. It was true that she hadn't time for a man like him. But he couldn't be more wrong about her. What would his reaction be if he knew what she did in her spare time? She imagined his eyes opening wide with shock, his loose-lipped mouth sagging, and she hid a secret smile.

She was tempted to enlighten Danvers, but resisted the urge. He was an important client for PrimeLight – hence the personal attention – and she gave no indication of her dislike.

'Good afternoon, Mr Danvers,' she said politely, moving towards the door. 'I'll send you the catalogue proofs as soon as they come into the office.'

The heels of her shoes beat a tattoo on the bleached oak floor-boards. She breathed a sigh of relief as the

2

smoked-glass doors slid shut behind her. Danvers was the last client she had to see that day. Heading towards the lift, she found thoughts of Danvers and PrimeLight fading from her mind. She had something far more important to think about.

As the lift descended swiftly and silently to the ground floor, she glanced at her wrist-watch. Five-thirty, hardly worth going back to her office. She decided to go straight back to her flat in Primrose Hill.

The early evening sunlight streamed through the windscreen as she nosed her BMW through the London traffic. The car crawled up Kingsway and was brought to a halt in a queue along Southampton Row. She slid the window down, liking the predictability of the voices raised in anger, screeching brakes, and the hooting of car horns, all of them floating towards her from a distance.

The smell of hot tar and exhaust fumes tickled her nostrils. Dear old rush-hour London. It would be many minutes before the traffic began to move. Picking up the car phone, she took the opportunity to contact her personal assistant.

'Gwen. I'm on my way home, or to be more accurate I'm sitting in the usual snarl-up along Southampton Row. Any messages?'

'Nothing important. How did it go with Danvers?'

Marika laughed. 'Predictably. No problems. He gave me a present of some underwear. I haven't looked at it yet.'

Gwen whistled. 'Took a fancy to you, did he? What's he like?'

'Overweight, balding, and thinks he's God's gift. He's his own number one fan.'

Gwen chuckled. 'Sounds just my type – not.'

'Ditto. Have a good weekend, Gwen. I should be back from my trip to France by Monday. If I need to stay on longer, I'll call you.'

She rang off, a frisson of anticipation prickling her skin as she thought about the package which had arrived in the post that morning. The auction catalogue had a plain cover, a glossy and tasteful deep-red. It was beautifully presented, each item listed and described in detail. On the back was a number embossed in gold, marking it out as an exclusive limited edition. Plainly, the catalogue itself was a collector's item.

She'd had time only to scan the first few pages and glance at the letter accompanying the catalogue before she left for work. Opening her briefcase, which lay on the seat beside her, she took out the folded sheet of embossed notepaper.

My dear, the letter began – the Major had begun to call her that of late, but she was under no illusions about her relationship with him; this assignment was to be strictly business – *I think you are ready to handle this transaction for me. Enclosed are details of your travel arrangements. As to the auction, you will see that I have marked the items in the catalogue which I wish you to bid for. It is most important that these books are added to the collection. I am relying on you.*

The Major went to give details of what she could expect of her weekend at the Ronsard Château in the Loire Valley. There would be ample opportunity to socialise at a garden party and ball – and to weigh-up the opposition, she read between the lines. He ended the letter by telling her to enjoy herself.

She knew what that meant too. There would be erotic possibilities which she was free to explore at will. Marika slipped the letter into the pocket of her wool jacket.

This was the first time that the Major had asked her to undertake a commission on his behalf. For two evenings a week she had been going to his house in Hampstead, studying the wealth of information about the main collections of erotica in the world.

For this the Major paid her a handsome retainer and

4

now it seemed she was to earn her money. The fee he named in his letter was very generous, but it wasn't just the money that made the idea of acting on his behalf so appealing. Nothing that involved the Discipline of Pearls was ever predictable. Belonging to the secret society had changed her perceptions and opened up to her a world of pleasure which she had not known existed.

The traffic began to edge forward and Marika slid the car into gear. Slipping a CD into the player, she listened to the haunting strains of a saxophone as the intro to 'Baker Street' filled the car. It was a song that always made her nostalgic and set her thinking of long sunny days.

As Gerry Rafferty began to sing, she was conscious that the dull glow of excitement inside her was intensifying.

Marika folded clothes into a small suitcase. Her passport and foreign currency were kept ready for speedy departures and her travel preparations were soon complete.

Her newly-washed hair brushed against her shoulders as she slipped out of her kimono. Walking over to the wardrobe mirror she ran a critical eye over her naked body. She knew that she was in good shape. Running a hand down either side of her body, she smoothed her palm over the indentation of her waist and the slight flare over her hip. Her nipples gathered as she cupped her breasts and she looked at them with pleasure.

Once she had been self-conscious because her nipples were dark and prominent – unusual in someone of her fair colouring. It was almost impossible for her to go bra-less when wearing light-coloured clothing, unless she wanted to make a statement. Her nipples were also incredibly sensitive, but that was something which she now regarded as a plus. She was proud of her ability to enjoy sex. In every respect she was a sensual being.

Her stomach was flat, sloping down to the light frosting of brownish hair at her groin. Perhaps her thighs were a little heavy, but her legs were long and any imperfection was hardly noticeable. On the whole she was pleased with her looks.

What woman was ever totally satisfied with her appearance?

She grinned at herself. 'You'll do. There've been no complaints so far.' In fact the opposite was true, she thought with a trace of satisfaction.

About to dress, she remembered Danvers's gift. Lifting the lid of the white box she parted the folds of printed tissue paper. Danvers might be obnoxious, but he had impeccable taste. The new design was gorgeous. She smiled thinly. He had also been right about her measurements.

The coffee lace basque was banded with insets of plain silk. It fitted her perfectly, the quarter cups moulding her breasts and easing them together. After putting on the matching G-string, she smoothed on the sheeny, lace-topped stockings.

She twirled in front of the mirror, delighted with the new underwear. The coffee set off the natural creaminess of her skin and the superb fit of the garments accentuated her curves. She felt the beginnings of a subtle erotic tension in the tingling of her skin, a certain tightness of her muscles. As she moved, her nipples pushed against the lace of the basque and the thong of her G-string rubbed slightly against the tender flesh on the insides of her buttocks.

It was some time since her last sexual encounter and she felt more body conscious than usual. The thought of the coming weekend filled her with a pleasant anticipation. She knew that she was likely to be mixing with some powerful individuals – people who were attractive, extremely wealthy and used to getting what they wanted. Such specialised collectors were refined individuals with honed tastes and a great capacity for personal indulgence.

The feeling of being erotically charged was pleasant and she decided to do nothing to relieve it. She bent forward to pull on a suede, sarong style skirt and the weight of her breasts shifted against the quarter cups and her cleavage deepened. Tucking a light-green silk blouse into her skirt, she slipped her feet into plain courts. Almost ready. She rang for a taxi. While she waited for it to arrive, she swept her hair into a French pleat.

Just before she left the flat, she slipped the pendant over her head and tucked it inside her blouse. She traced the outline of the pearls and the newly carved diamond motif, feeling the hollows and ridges on the jet oval through the thin fabric of her blouse.

Six months ago a man – whom she had come to know as Jordan Stone – had approached her in the car park under her Dockland office and given her a pendant. Since then her life had changed dramatically – was changing still. It amused her to think that she had almost refused to accept Stone's gift. Now she knew that the pendant was a passport to singular pleasures.

The gold chain felt cold against her skin, but it soon grew warm from her body heat.

Chapter Two

THE FLIGHT WAS uneventful and it was nearing midnight when the plane set down in Paris. A sleek black Daimler was waiting for Marika outside Charles de Gaulle. The chauffeur was young and good-looking. He smiled as he opened the door for her, then stowed her suitcase in the boot.

'Good evening, mademoiselle.'

'Good evening.'

Marika allowed herself to sink back against the leather seats as the car drew away from the airport. They headed for the Boulevard Peripherique and picked up the A10 motorway which led to Orleans.

For a while she looked out of the tinted windows as the car slipped smoothly through the night. The flashes of light as traffic passed them on the opposite carriageway were hypnotic and she found her eyelids drooping. There was only the purr of the powerful engine and the faint rumble of passing cars.

She fell into a light doze and when she woke they were leaving the outskirts of Orleans. Shuttered streets and brightly-lit shop fronts sped by. Somehow she had slept away an hour or more. They sped on for a while, until they exited from a featureless motorway and headed west. In another ten minutes they approached

Beaugency, a small town which sloped steeply down to a sixteenth-century bridge over the Loire. Looming above the darkened streets, Marika could see the spires of a church and the bulk of a huge Norman tower.

The car turned onto a narrow country road and the lights of Beaugency faded behind them. Marika sensed that they were nearing the end of their journey. She sat upright, scanning the night-shadowed fields. Huge trees seemed to loom out of the darkness as the car slowed and then drew to a halt in front of a pair of enormous iron gates. A coat of arms adorned the centre of the gate, which opened inwards to allow them access.

Marika's eyes widened as the Ronsard Château came into view. It was far larger and grander than she had expected – a fairy tale vision of white stone, its pointed turrets and parapets reflected in the waters of a moat. Light blazed from every window. They drove along an avenue of pleached limes which cut through formal gardens on both sides. Drawing up on a circular gravelled drive, the Daimler drew to a halt beside a number of beautiful glossy cars.

Other guests were just arriving. Liveried footmen moved to and fro amongst the cars. Marika saw a tall, slim man with iron grey hair get out of a white Rolls Royce. Against the white of his shirt his lean face looked deeply tanned. His dark suit was impeccably tailored and she caught the glint of a diamond tie-pin. The man glanced at her, his severe features lifting in a smile of appreciation.

Marika smiled and looked away, then because she sensed that he hadn't moved, she looked at him again. He was certainly handsome and there was an arrogant sensuality about him. He was standing perfectly still, his eyes holding an expression of complete absorption.

Something about him made her uneasy. Perhaps it

9

was the fact that he did not care that people were turning their heads to look at them both, knowing smiles on their faces. Or perhaps it was the way he was looking at – almost studying her, with the cool dispassionate glance of the hunter weighing up its prey.

She felt the heat flood her cheeks as the man continued to stare. Now he was being rude. This was becoming embarrassing. Breaking eye contact with him she began walking towards the Château. As she mounted the steps which led to an ornate front door, she sensed that he was waiting for her to look around. Denying him that small victory, she resisted looking over her shoulder.

Marika hurried into the shelter of the doorway. She was annoyed with herself for being rattled. After all, the man had only looked at her. But the fact remained that she had been deeply affected by him. At some instinctive level, he made her afraid – and she didn't like that, not one little bit.

The chauffeur deposited her case on the top step, where a footman retrieved it. 'Will you come this way, mademoiselle?' the footman said and Marika followed him into the entrance hall.

She gained an impression of studied opulence as she walked across the vaulted room. Chandeliers blazed and every surface seemed covered with gilded scroll-work and shell motifs. Lavishly framed mirrors reflected multi-angled views of the room. Her heels echoed on the marble floor as she followed the footman towards a staircase which led in a graceful curve to an upper floor. The footman stopped and opened a pair of gilded double doors.

'This is your room, mademoiselle.'

Marika thanked him and stepped into the room. She looked around in astonishment. A huge, satin-draped four-poster bed was set against one wall. Brocade covered sofas and chairs, exquisite gilded tables, and decorated cabinets were set around the room. In one corner there was a marble plinth topped by a huge gilded vase from which frothed masses of creamy bourbon roses.

The footman left the room, closing the doors silently behind him. Marika walked slowly around, absorbing the beauty of the room. It was only when she sat down in front of the dressing table that she noticed the letter propped up against the cut glass perfume bottles and antique enamelled boxes.

Opening the envelope, she read, *Welcome Mademoiselle Fremen. Please make yourself comfortable. If you need something, anything at all, ring the bell next to the bed. Your every need will be attended to. While you are here at the Ronsard Château you must not lift a finger to help yourself. I hope you sleep well. Your host will introduce himself to you and your fellow guests after breakfast tomorrow.*

There was no signature. Marika smiled. The whole situation was like a fantasy. This château was unbelievable – the fabulous decor, the liveried footmen. She felt as if she had stepped on to the film set of *Valmont*.

Glancing at her watch she saw that it was nearing two a.m. After dozing in the car she did not feel tired, so she decided to ring for some tea and then to have a bath. Picking up the bell-rope next to the bed she gave it three sharp tugs.

She was unpacking her case when the knock came at the door. Without turning around she said, 'Come in.'

The door opened and closed. Marika glanced over her shoulder and the smile froze on her face. Standing with his back to the door was the distinguished grey-haired man she had seen as she arrived.

'What the hell are you doing in my room?' she said, annoyed that her voice shook a little.

'Did you not ring for service?' His voice was

11

cultured and well-modulated.

'Well . . . . yes. But I expected a maid.'

'And now you have me. Do not be alarmed. This is to be no ordinary weekend, as you will soon find out. Allow me to introduce myself. Charles Germain – at your service.'

His mouth twitched and Marika found herself responding to the dry humour in his words. The situation seemed so ridiculous, but then she was used to surprises when on society business. Charles, was it? He was certainly a most unusual 'maid'. He looked far less alarming close to, the smile lightening the severity of his features.

He had blue eyes which glittered against his tanned skin. His mouth was wide and firm and his lips were parted to show very white teeth.

'I *was* ringing to ask for some tea,' she said trying to sound serious, but she couldn't keep up the façade of disapproval. She felt very close to laughter.

'That wasn't the service I had in mind.'

'No, I didn't think it was.'

It was easy to talk to him, to slip into the light banter that attractive women exchanged with personable men. She found herself wondering why she had been so disquieted by their meeting outside the Château. This handsome, mature man was very attractive.

Then Charles's smile faded and she felt a prickle of apprehension. There it was again, the underlying coldness, the penetrative quality of his light blue eyes. His stillness, that air of absolute self-possession was hypnotic. She felt unable to look away, to break free from that calm unwavering gaze.

'Unbutton your blouse,' he said softly.

'I beg your pardon . . .' she stammered, thinking she hadn't heard him correctly.

He grinned and his face was suddenly boyish again. He looked as if he had been caught out playing a prank. The chameleon quality of him confused her. Was he playing with her? She couldn't tell whether he was dangerous or just amusing himself at her expense.

'You are very beautiful, Miss Fremen,' he said evenly. 'May I call you Marika?'

'How do you know my name?'

The seconds passed while he looked at her with undisguised admiration and the moment for outrage passed too.

'Since you haven't screamed for help, or told me to get the hell out, then I must assume that you intend to comply. So – unbutton your blouse . . . please. And let me assure you that I am not in the habit of explaining myself or qualifying any request I make.'

Marika sensed that he spoke the truth. This was a man who was used to giving orders and having them obeyed. She was annoyed by his arrogance, but also aware of a dull throbbing at the base of her belly. Dammit, she was beginning to find his presence exciting. The situation had an air of the unknown about it, reminding her of the other times when she had responded to the challenge implicit in a black card with a telephone number printed in raised gold lettering. But that had been early on, when she was a rookie, a fledgling member, and her suitability for membership was being tested.

She decided to go along with him for the time being, wanting to see how far he would go. He probably expected outrage or resistance. Was that the kick for him?

Lifting her chin, she held his gaze as she reached up and undid the top three buttons of her blouse. Slowly she spread apart the 'V' formed by the open revers of her blouse and exposed the creamy skin of her throat and upper chest.

'Now what?' she said coolly.

Charles moved closer, his eyes glittering at her show

of spirit. She steeled herself not to take a step back. The edge of the bed was only inches from the back of her thighs. If she moved even slightly she would overbalance and fall backwards.

Stopping directly in front of her, Charles stretched out his hand and ran a finger and thumb over each of her collar bones. Marika suppressed a shiver as the tips of his fingers brushed against her skin, his touch as light as butterfly wings.

Dipping one finger into her blouse opening, Charles's fingers moved down to the swell of her cleavage. She found that she was anticipating the touch of his hands on her breasts and they tingled with readiness inside the quarter cups of the basque. Her nipples gathered, pressing against the flimsy lace. Surely Charles could see the tiny peaks under her blouse. But he ignored her breasts, only hooking two fingers around the gold chain and drawing the pendant free.

'As I thought,' he said with satisfaction, looking down at the pearl-encircled oval that lay in his palm. 'You had to be the Major's agent. I knew he would send someone if he could not come himself. I approve of his choice.'

'You know the Major?' she said.

He grinned and there was something hard and unreadable in his voice. 'Oh, yes. I know him. And I know all about the Discipline of Pearls . . . and the rules. Members of the society are very strict about following the rules, are they not?'

She nodded. It all made sense now – the way he had appeared in her room, his arrogance, his proprietary attitude. He must be a member of the society too. Perhaps he was also an elder – one of the powerful and privileged few – like the Major.

His nearness was exciting. She could smell his cologne and the fainter scent of clean maleness. The fact that she hadn't been this close to a handsome man for some weeks was suddenly uppermost in her mind.

'Would you say that coming here for the weekend is in the nature of an assignment?' he asked.

'I suppose so,' she said, seeing the way that his mind was working and feeling the tight little knot of excitement in her belly begin to loosen and spread heat through her loins.

Inside the crotch of her G-string her sex fluttered and grew damp. Charles knew the effect he was having on her, she was sure of it. She knew also that it amused him. She felt annoyed with herself for responding so readily to him, but she couldn't help it. Her body was running on ahead of her. The sexual tension which had surfaced within her whilst she was dressing in her London flat, began to bubble and fizz.

'Then by accepting this "assignment" for the Major you have professed your willingness to abide by the laws of obedience?' Charles said, his voice maddeningly calm while his blue eyes bored into her.

She found that she could not look away. Her breasts were swollen now, the nipples hard and aching inside the confinement of the basque, and the crotch of her G-string felt definitely wetter.

'I thought so,' he said, although she had not answered him. 'And how far have you risen, my dear? I suspect that you aren't a newcomer to the society.'

'I hold a position of some responsibility,' she said. 'I make my own choices and don't have to wait for a black card to arrive through the post. And I'm no longer obliged to pick up the telephone and go off on an assignment which has been arranged for someone else's pleasure.'

'Really? But I think you miss that, don't you?'

Bringing up both hands, he pushed firmly against her shoulders. Staggering back a step, Marika lost her balance and fell onto the bed. The breath left her in a

15

whoosh as she slammed onto the satin bedcover and her legs were revealed to the thigh by the split in her sarong skirt. She began to push herself up by her elbows, a protest rising to her lips.

'Keep still.'

It was said evenly, with the absolute surety of being obeyed. He didn't raise his voice.

He didn't need to, Marika thought, part of her rebelling even as she obeyed him. Clenching her hands into fists, she pressed them into the cool satin of the cover.

Charles stepped between her spread knees and she felt the rough warmth of his expensive trousers through her sheeny stockings. He stood looking down on her, his sexual tension palpable in every line of his body.

'You really are beautiful,' he said as he ran his hands up the outside of her legs. 'And what a challenge. Those who are strong-willed are the sweetest when they allow themselves to surrender. Be still now. I want to enjoy you.'

Torn between outrage and desire she stayed as she was, her upper body propped up so that she was looking down and watching his strong brown hands push her skirt up to her waist. Somehow she felt more naked than if she had been undressed completely.

With the butter-soft suede bunched around her waist her hips and legs looked vulnerable and exposed. She was conscious of the strip of pale belly between the edge of the basque and top of her G-string. Charles's grip slid inwards and she felt his hands on the bare flesh above her lace stocking-tops. Her breath left her in a gasp when the backs of his fingers brushed almost casually against the triangle of coffee lace covering her pubis.

Rubbing gently with his knuckles he stroked against the fabric until the referred pressure caused her clitoris to throb and burn. Shamed by the heat that flooded her cheeks and by the way she strained towards his hand, Marika closed her eyes.

'Open them,' Charles demanded. 'I want to watch you come. Obedience, remember? Haven't you learned your lessons well?'

Oh yes, she had learned well. She knew about the power struggles between two sexual partners, that obedience was inherent in the acceptance of any assignment within the secret society – and he knew that too. He seemed to know all about the apprenticeship she had served and she felt as if part of her soul had been peeled away.

That knowledge gave him power over her and she shuddered with excitement. The willing submission flooded her body, freeing her to experience pleasure in her shame and whatever else he would ask of her.

'I said, open your eyes. And open your body to me. Part your thighs, Marika.'

The pressure of his hands increased and she felt her thighs part and her lace-covered sex open to him. A trickle of wetness slid out of her swollen labia and she moaned under her breath. Her body wanted him, but there was still some mental resistance. It was always this way with her. She wanted the loss of control, the spiked pleasure of being dominated, but the strong independent-woman side of her fought against it.

Forcing herself to open her eyes, she found that he was leaning forward slightly, his face closer now so that she could see the white lines radiating out from the corners of his eyes. He had moved slightly and she felt the hardness of his erection pressing into her soft inner thigh.

Charles glanced down her body and then back up to her face, as if it was her mind he desired to plunder. Despite his arousal, his blue eyes were cold and calculating. And then she knew the source of her fear.

17

This man wanted more than sex from her. He wanted to control her, to get inside her head. But the realisation was all muddled up with the tension and the pleasure. She couldn't think clearly. Her body, so used to receiving pleasure, was clamouring for release. His strong brown fingers kneaded the soft skin of her thighs and moved in towards the hot pulsing centre of her.

'That's it, Marika. Give it all to me.'

'I can't . . .' she whispered, knowing that she lied.

He laughed softly as he slipped both thumbs under the edge of the G-string and stroked the light brown curls.

'Oh, but you can.'

Finding the pouting lips of her sex, he smoothed them apart flattening her folds so that the damp lace brushed against her swollen bud. The soft caress of the lace as it grazed the tender throbbing morsel teased her to a more intense arousal.

She could hardly stand it. Any moment she would break and dissolve. But although the sensations built and her thigh muscles trembled with tension she did not come. Charles knew just how to vary the pressure, so that she was brought to the crest of an orgasm but not swept over the edge.

As her hips began to work beyond her control, he used his thumbs to rub either side of her straining bud, flicking the exposed tip every now and then until she moaned with desperation. Her vagina was hot and slick and the G-string was soaking with her creamy juices.

'Please . . .' she whimpered, wanting, needing to have him inside her. She yearned to be naked under him – to feel his lips on hers, his hands clutching at her hips while he surged inside her – and was certain that he knew this too, but he deliberately held back from taking her.

'So impatient,' he said coolly. 'I want to watch you . . . this time. I want to take your orgasm for my own.'

She shuddered deep inside. How dreadful it was to have him watching her expression, to demand to see her blushes, to own every minute evidence of her pleasure. She felt insulted that he ignored her mouth – did not want her tight swollen nipples. Her eager wet sex was ignored too, left bereft, while all the time in a ceaseless hypnotic rhythm his clever fingers stroked and rubbed her slippery flesh and brought her to the trembling brink of a clitoral explosion.

He demanded to have control over her responses, forced her to enjoy what he did, and everything in her resisted the basic primal urge to give in to him completely. She might desire this man, but she did not like him. And that made the situation all the more devastating. Marika chewed at her lower lip, agonised by the fact that in some strange way her resistance to Charles increased the erotic tension.

Collapsing backwards, her head tossing from side to side, she could think of nothing but his fingers which were circling her clitoris spreading her wetness over and over it. As he lifted the triangle of lace away from her sex and used two fingers to slide up her open wet folds and pinch the scrap of pulsing flesh firmly between a finger and thumb, she cried out.

Oh God, she couldn't hold back. She was going to come.

Her eyes opened wide and she grunted and spasmed, her legs thrashing as an incredibly intense orgasm ripped through her. At the moment when the pleasure peaked Charles thrust two fingers into her and rotated them against her fleshy walls. Hooking his fingers he pressed against the sensitive pad behind her pubic bone.

Marika mouthed the back of her hand, stifling her moans as her climax went on and on. Charles used his fingers like a cock, the tips brushing against her womb. Bearing down on his hand she ground herself against him. Somehow this was more intimate and more shocking than having his cock inside her. She felt used, manipulated – a helpless thing of pleasure.

When she came back to herself she found that Charles was still bent over her, watching the tension slide from her features. His face was relaxed and he looked almost gentle. She felt a moment of tenderness towards him and reached out her arms for him.

He grinned, but as before the smile did not reach his eyes.

'No need to ask if it was good. You're a natural wanton. You resist, but you cannot help enjoying being forced. It takes a certain strength of character to give yourself up to that kind of pleasure. The act of submission is so often misunderstood by those who like to preach morals to others.'

She smiled, impressed by his perception. Stretching her arms above her head, she arched her back provocatively.

'Mmmm. I've been well-trained by a master of self-control. It *was* good. But that's not all I enjoy. I'm not hooked on submission. I'm just as able to take the initiative. Give me your cock now. Let me pleasure you. I can promise you'll enjoy it.'

Charles moved backwards, his severely handsome face hardening. Was it the mention of another lover – someone as strong as he – which had displeased him? Or was it the fact that she had shown her claws? Glancing down at her, he said coolly, 'Not this time. I've had what I came for. I wanted to see whether you took your position within the Discipline of Pearls seriously. The Major would be proud of your devotion to pleasure. Good night, Marika. Sleep well.'

Before she could protest, he strode to the door and let himself out of her room. Marika watched him go, hardly able to believe what had just happened between them. She knew that he had been excited by her responses – hadn't she felt his erect cock against her inner thigh? – yet he had walked away without a backward glance. It took a great deal of self-control to do that or an insufferable arrogance.

Pushing down her skirt she got up and went to the en suite bathroom. Her body tingled with repletion and yet she was somehow unsatisfied. She didn't know how to feel about Charles. Part of her was insulted by his cavalier handling of her, but another darker part was fascinated by him.

There had been other lovers within the society, all of them individual in their sexual proclivities, but no one had been like Charles. It rather frightened her to think that she had allowed herself to be manipulated into experiencing the most mind-blowing orgasm at his hands – thrashing and moaning to order, while he had been able to remain aloof and be largely unmoved by the whole thing.

He hadn't even undressed her or looked at her body, yet he had compelled her to perform for him.

Charles Germain was a strange man indeed. As she stripped off her clothes and turned on the shower, she found herself looking forward with some consternation to their next meeting.

Chapter Three

MARIKA DRESSED CAREFULLY in a white organza shirt and well-cut black trousers, before descending the staircase to the ground floor next morning. A wide black belt emphasised her slim waist and her hair was secured at her nape with a black ribbon. Chunky silver jewellery completed her outfit.

An impeccably uniformed footman directed her to the dining room where the other guests were having breakfast.

Sunlight streamed in through floor-length windows, hung with swathes of white and gold striped silk. Through the glass she could see a formal terrace. Marigolds and geraniums spilled from huge stone urns which topped the coping of a balustrade. Beyond that there was a vista of sweeping lawns, paved walkways, and mature trees. In the distance there was the metallic glint of a lake.

A number of tables had been placed alongside the open windows. Most of the tables were occupied. She saw Charles at once. He was sitting with a sharply-dressed man and a dark-haired woman wearing a fitted red dress. Their conversation was animated and the woman's laughter fluted across the room as Marika took her place at an empty table nearby.

Charles looked up and nodded politely, his expression pleasant and neutral.

'Good morning,' he said coolly.

Marika replied in the same tone, thinking that no one could have guessed what had taken place between them. The man with Charles smiled at her, his eyes sharpening with interest. He was around thirty and very good-looking in a well-groomed, boyish sort of way. His hair was dark and worn fashionably long and his skin was the colour of caramel. Marika thought he looked like a sportsman, perhaps a footballer.

As the 'footballer' continued to stare openly at Marika, the woman in red glared at him and hissed something under her breath. She hunched her rather bony shoulders and stabbed at the air with one finger, as if punctuating every word.

Definitely the possessive type, Marika thought with amusement, wondering what Charles was making of the altercation. The 'footballer' turned his attention back to his companion, patting her hand placatingly. The smile the dark-haired woman gave him would have frozen salt water.

Marika ordered coffee and croissants and ate her breakfast alone, content to look around the room and familiarise herself with the other guests. The room gradually filled and a low buzz of well-bred conversation and the clink of monogrammed cutlery rose on the air. She was surprised to see so many guests. There must be at least fifty of them staying at the Château. Possibly others would be arriving for the auction. Obviously the different lots were very sought after.

After breakfast the guests began to move into the drawing room where trays of fresh coffee and soft drinks were set out. Marika found Charles at her side. He looked relaxed in a cream linen suit.

'Did you sleep well?' he asked.

'Very well. I always do after an orgasm,' she replied blithely. 'And you?'

If Charles was surprised he didn't show it.

'Those of clear conscience always sleep well,' he said smoothly. 'Ah, here is our host. It seems that this is the official viewing time for the private guests. I see that you didn't bring your catalogue with you. You may share mine if you wish.'

She smiled. 'Thank you, but that won't be necessary. I know which items interest me.'

'As you wish.' She felt his hand in the small of her back as he escorted her through the double doors. The heat of his fingers seeped through her blouse and she thought of those same fingers on her sex the night before, spreading her silky wet flesh open, stroking her to a shattering climax.

Her skin prickled at the remembered pleasure and she felt herself growing moist and her pulses quickening. Why was it that she responded so readily to Charles? She did not even like him very much. He was too detached, too sure of his own charm and strength of character. Yet there was some indefinable attraction between them. She determined to concentrate on her assignment. Shape-up now, you're a professional, she told herself. With that in mind, she dragged her thoughts back to the present.

A tall man with strong features and swept-back brown hair entered the room. He wore an Italian suit in chocolate-coloured linen over a white silk shirt. Marika judged him to be in his late forties, but it was difficult to tell. His broad shoulders and muscular frame might have belonged to a much younger man.

After introducing himself as Alain Cartier – the new Duc de Ronsard – and giving a few words of formal welcome, he said, 'I'm sure that you are all eager to view my late father's collection. It is with the utmost regret that I have arranged this auction, but I'm sure

24

that you are all aware of my position. Such an estate is very expensive to maintain . . .' He shrugged and spread his hands in an eloquent gesture. 'There is some comfort for me in knowing that this collection, of which my father was so proud, will be going to others who appreciate the sensuality and beauty of works of erotica. Some of these books are unique, others are rare editions, all of them are extremely collectable. But you do not need me to tell you that. You all know my father's reputation for being one of *the* great collectors of erotica.'

He paused and smiled. There was a ripple of polite applause. The Duc held up his hand in acknowledgement of his guests' sympathy and respect.

'So. Let us begin,' he went on. 'If you would all face the end of the room.'

Marika decided that she liked Alain Cartier. He was not conventionally good-looking, but there was an attractive tilt to his eyes and a self-effacing air to him which was endearing.

A number of footmen entered the room and stood by while Alain unlocked the doors of the floor-length cabinets which filled one complete wall. The open doors revealed crammed book shelves.

'Please browse at will, but I must insist that you wear the cotton gloves provided. Many of these works are old and fragile. My servants will remain for security purposes, but I'm afraid that I have business to attend to. Will you all excuse me? I hope to be able to join you for the garden party, this afternoon.'

'A charming man, the Duc, is he not?' Charles whispered to Marika.

'Very,' she answered, more aware than she cared to be of the warmth of his breath against her neck. He smelt of cinnamon cigarettes. 'It's a pity that he's having to sell off part of his inheritance.'

Charles shrugged. 'If the old Duc had spent less on

his collection the estate would be in better shape. But then I can understand how the old man became obsessed with acquiring the rarest books.' He looked closely at Marika. 'The quest for pleasure can be all-consuming. Don't you agree?'

Marika smiled dismissively and did not answer. Charles spoke lightly, but Marika felt again the underlying intensity of the man. It was as if something was coiled inside him, something deep and dark that was kept on a leash.

'Coward. Have you no answer for me?' Charles said under his breath as she moved away and took a pair of gloves from the tray held by one of the footmen.

She did not take up his challenge. Let him think what he liked about her. She had nothing to prove. In a moment Charles, having donned the gloves, appeared beside her at the first cabinet. There were already gaps amongst the rows of books. Prospective buyers were sitting on sofas leafing through open volumes. Now and then she heard a murmur of appreciation.

Someone said, in a stage whisper, 'But my dear, this work is priceless. I *must* have it.'

There was an air of expectation and tension in the room. Little huddles of people were grouped around a particularly fine work. Marika began to get caught up in the general interest. The auction itself promised to be quite something.

Taking a list from the pocket of her trousers Marika began looking for the books the Major had told her to acquire. Although she tried to concentrate on the task in hand she could not help but be aware of Charles's proximity. The force of his presence surrounded her like a perfume, heady, musky and more than a little dangerous.

She felt a soft touch against her hair as Charles leaned close and peered over her shoulder. She felt the urge to lay the list flat against her chest, hiding the contents of it from him. But the gesture seemed childish. Charles would learn soon enough which books she was particularly interested in.

'Hmmm. The Major's taste is impeccable. The first edition De Sade and the original manuscript of a Sacher-Masoch, amongst others? Those two alone would be the pride of any collection. You'll need to strike a hard bargain to get them.'

She turned around, a confident smile on her lips.

'I can handle that.'

Charles raised his eyebrows. 'Perhaps. But almost everyone here will be after the same items. Do you see that Japanese man? He has more money than you could ever dream of. That one over there? He's the agent for an Arabian oil magnate. Believe me, if you are not to return empty-handed, you will need my help.'

Marika was annoyed by his certainty that she would fail. Just who did he think he was?

'If you are so wary of the opposition, what makes you think that you'll be able to out-bid everyone? I suppose your money's in gold, diamonds, or . . . uranium?' she faltered, trying to think of the world's most expensive commodities.

He nodded. 'Spot on. All of those and more. My family have been merchant bankers for three generations.'

She tried not to look impressed, more determined than ever now to succeed by her own merits. Somehow Charles had a way of making her feel gauche and unsure of herself. She had done her 'homework' before coming to the Château and so knew the background and financial status of most of the prospective guests, but there had been no mention of any Charles Germain. With him, she had no choice but to trust her instincts. The trouble was, her instincts were telling her to avoid him while her body was crying out for his touch.

Reaching into the cabinet she took out a slip-case containing a handmade folder, beautifully half-bound in vellum and Mingei paper.

Pointedly ignoring Charles she walked past him towards one of the exquisitely upholstered sofas. She heard Charles's softly mocking laugh as she sat down and began to examine the folder of amorous drawings by the Marquis Von Bayros. The art nouveau prints were exquisite, but the delicate lines and flesh tones seemed to swim before her eyes. Damn Charles. She could not concentrate with him hovering nearby.

She was about to move to another seat when Charles, holding a green, cloth-bound volume in his hands, walked past the back of her sofa on his way across the room. Bending down he rested one arm on the sofa back and whispered to her.

'I realise that you find my company charming and will be devastated that I have to leave you briefly, but I'm afraid that you will have to excuse me. My friends are waiting for me over there.'

He indicated a sofa, set between two marble pillars. Marika saw the couple Charles had been with at breakfast. The man waved and the dark-haired woman raised her chin and threw a look of pure malice at Marika.

'I don't think one of your friends likes me very much,' Marika said.

Charles smiled. 'Greta? Ah, she sees every beautiful woman as a threat to herself. The man she is with is quite a celebrity in his own country and many women pursue him. Poor Greta, she is very insecure and needs lots of attention to reassure her that she too is beautiful and desirable, you understand?'

Marika thought that she understood only too well. No doubt Charles was more than willing to 'reassure' Greta.

'It's the first time I've heard it called that,' she said evenly.

28

'Pardon me?'

'Reassurance.'

Charles smiled, his blue eyes flashing with humour. 'Wit as well as beauty,' he said. 'I'm more sorry than ever that I won't be at the garden party this afternoon. Unfortunately I have a ... previous engagement, which I cannot break. My special services are required and I can never resist a heartfelt plea. But I shall look forward very much to seeing you at the masked ball tonight.'

He reached for her hand and brought it to his lips. The old-fashioned gesture was charming and her stomach flipped as his warm lips brushed her skin.

She knew with absolute certainty that Charles's 'engagement' involved sex. And she knew also that it was Greta who was to be at the centre of some specially orchestrated scenario. The brief flare of jealousy she experienced was unexpected and unwanted.

Dammit. She was here primarily to do a job. Any sexual liaisons, although pleasant, were meant to be brief, pleasurable interludes – the icing on a sumptuous gateau of indulgence. The last thing she wanted was to form any attachments. But it seemed as if Charles Germain had other ideas about that, and he was not a man to be put off easily.

A large marquee had been erected on the velvet perfection of the back lawn. Liveried footmen moved to and fro serving the guests with drinks and canapés.

The guests were clustered in groups. The Duc moved amongst them exchanging a word here and there. Marika found Alain Cartier pleasant and with impeccable manners, but he had the slightly distracted air of a man who was absorbed by the amount of money he would be making over the weekend.

29

As the Duc moved away and continued on his rounds, Marika helped herself to a tiny pastry piled high with caviare. It was delicious, the caviar bursting saltily on her tongue as she chewed.

'These are very good, are they not?' said a softly-accented voice at her side.

Marika turned her head, agreeing that they were, and saw Charles's male companion from breakfast.

'Permit me to introduce myself,' the man said. 'I am Juan Perez Aparicio. Perhaps you have heard of me? Many newspapers have run features on me, as I have retired from playing polo and am setting up a business in your country. Which is lucky for me, or I would not be here beside you now.'

Not football then, as she had thought, but she had been right about Juan having been a sportsman. Close-up the man was even better looking. He had liquid brown eyes, a straight nose, and smooth skin the exact colour of vanilla fudge. His dark hair was slicked back and clasped at his nape.

Juan complimented Marika on her outfit and matching hat while he undressed her with his eyes. Marika felt a twinge of pity for Greta. It was not surprising that she felt insecure. This man was a wolf of the first order.

'Marika Fremen,' she said coolly. 'And I'm afraid that I haven't heard of you. Perhaps I've been reading the wrong newspapers.'

He laughed and his handshake was firm, his fingers warm and strong. Cupping her elbow he began steering her through the guests. She felt mild annoyance that he assumed that she wanted his company, but he *was* the most interesting person in the immediate vicinity – as well as the most attractive. It might be amusing to flirt with him a little.

'May I?' he said, drawing her towards one of the paved walkways. 'It is cooler under the rose . . . What do you call this thing made of wood?'

'A pergola,' she said.

'Ah, a strange word. No matter. Will you sit with me? I would like to talk with you.'

Marika sat on a cast-iron bench which was shadowed by the profusion of roses. Huge blowzy heads of pink, white, and cream almost covered the pergola, their sweet, heady scent perfuming the air.

'So, Marika. You know Charles Germain,' Juan stated.

Marika sipped her Pouilly Fuissé. 'We are acquainted,' she said.

'Ah, you English are so – how do you say it? Understated.' He leaned close, not bothering to disguise his desire for her. 'I know about the society,' he said. 'So we may speak freely with each other. Greta and myself are members. Charles is a compelling man, is he not? No doubt he has already recruited you to our ranks.' He placed his hand gently on her knee. 'There is no need for us to go through the usual pretence and small-talk. Let us go to your room. I want to fuck you. I have been hard since the moment I first saw you. You will find me an excellent and tireless lover.'

Marika stared at him in astonishment. He seemed absolutely certain that she would agree. His hand crept higher, rucking up the filmy fabric of her skirt. He leaned over her, his sensual mouth curved in a confident smile.

She knocked his hand away and glared at him. There was something all wrong about this. It was not that Juan had come-on to her in such a crass way, it was the fact that he believed it was perfectly all right to do so. She was angry, but she was also amused and not a little curious.

'Show me your left hand,' she said coldly.

His smile wavered. 'What? But why? I don't

31

understand,' he protested, but he held his hand up for her to see.

As she had expected he wore no ring. Whatever society he was talking about it was not the Discipline of Pearls. All male members were required to wear their black-pearl rings at all times. There was some mystery here and Charles was apparently involved. She wanted to know more.

Marika stood up abruptly. 'Come with me,' she ordered, walking along the path towards the clipped green walls of a maze.

Juan followed eagerly. She hid a smile. He obviously thought that she had succumbed to his oh-so-obvious charms. She decided that he needed to be taught a lesson. Reaching the maze she took one of the paths which led off to one side and continued walking until they came upon a cul-de-sac.

She turned around to face Juan, placing her back against the statue of a satyr which formed a centre-piece in the enclosed space. Juan was visibly excited. His lips, with their petulant droop, were moist and full. They had an almost purple sheen to them and were parted to show his perfect white teeth.

'Here?' he said hoarsely. 'You do not care that someone might see us? Oh, you English. You are cool outside, but like the alley cat when aroused. You want Juan to put his big *palo* into you and ride you until you scream with pleasure. No?'

'No,' Marika said calmly. 'I want you to get down on your knees.'

Juan's face darkened. He looked less sure of himself. Then he grinned.

'Ah, you want to play games first? Very well.'

Still smiling, he sank to his knees, his trousers drawing tight over his strongly muscled thighs. His erection was prodigious. She could see it pressing against the fabric. He was very handsome with his broad shoulders and strong chest. Unzipping his trousers, Juan reached into his fly and drew out his cock.

'You like?' he said, stroking himself. 'I am a big boy. No?'

'Hmmm,' she murmured, for a boy he was; a spoilt child who thought only of himself and what he wanted.

Juan began working his shaft back and forth, smoothing the tight skin back from the big glans. He was so aroused that a drop of clear fluid emerged from the eye of his cock and trembled there, a perfect tear. Marika regarded him coolly, absorbing his pleased expression, his pride in his own potency.

After a moment she looked away from Juan's straining member and locked gazes with him. Slowly she eased up the skirt of her dress. She wore only a pair of panties under her dress. Juan's eyes followed her movements, widening when they took in her rounded thighs and the white, lace triangle that covered her pubis. Hooking her thumbs under the sides of her panties, Marika eased them down and stepped out of them.

Juan glanced at the scrap of white lace which lay on the gravel path and made a move to rise, but Marika stopped him with a gesture.

'Stay as you are. I have a task for you.'

'Stay?' he murmured, his full lips tightening mutinously, but he obeyed her.

She smiled inwardly, sensing that Juan was not used to taking orders from women. No doubt he had had his pick of any number of adoring fans. It would be interesting to see how he reacted to what she had in mind.

She moved backwards until she felt the coldness of the stone plinth against her naked buttocks. Holding her dress above her waist she rested her bottom

33

against the stone, arched her back, and parted her thighs. The muscles in her calves tautened as she braced the heels of her strappy sandals on the ground.

Juan gave a groan as his eyes fastened on the frosting of light brown curls at the juncture of her thighs. He inched towards her, uncaring of the gravel rubbing against his expensive trousers. Marika jiggled her bottom and opened her legs wider, letting him see the moist red lips of her sex and the shadowed mouth of her vagina.

'Well, Juan? I thought you were eager to do me a service,' she said coolly. 'Give me your mouth. It is so well-shaped and firm. Surely you know how to use it?'

Realisation dawned on Juan. He raised horrified eyes to her.

'You want that I should eat your pussy? But no. I do not do this thing. It is not fitting that a man should serve a woman in this way. I—'

'You will do as I say,' Marika cut in. 'Or go back to the party. Now. Use your mouth and tongue to give me pleasure. If you want your reward you have to work for it.'

Juan flinched at the tone of her voice, but she saw that his cheeks were flushed and his erection was even bigger than before. His strong reddish shaft twitched and pulsed as he moved. Above the rucked-up band of his silk boxers, his tight sac and mat of pubic hair looked as if it was being offered on a plate. Marika could feel the war within him – the sexual tension and wish to demonstrate his prowess was mixed with his fierce latin pride and his manly need to be in control.

For a moment she thought he would get up and go. The decision hung in the balance. Then Juan cursed softly.

'You are a strong woman. You English, you excite me,' he said as he placed one hand on each of Marika's hips and bent close.

She felt his warm lips nuzzling into her, feeling their way through her pubic curls. Then his tongue probed the warm, salt valley of her sex, tentatively at first then with more eagerness.

'That's it,' Marika said softly. 'Oh, yes. Just like that. You see, Juan, it's not so difficult to obey a woman, is it?'

He pulled away for a moment and looked up at her. His mouth was wet with her juices and there was a look of total absorption on his handsome face.

'No. It is not, Marika. You are wonderful,' he breathed. 'You taste like honey and musk on silk.'

'Taste me some more,' she said, the feeling of having power over this strong and vital man making her tremble with pleasure.

Juan obliged. He began licking upwards towards the apex of her sex-lips, the movement smoothing her clit free of its tiny hood. Marika sighed, letting the warm slippery sensations wash over her. There was a pulsing heat in her belly and she moaned softly and thrust her pubis towards Juan as he began to suck and lick her in earnest.

He might have been slow to start with, but he was more than making up for that now. His tongue lolled against her swollen flesh, playing up and down the sides of her clit. He used his lips to nibble the throbbing morsel, sucking it gently and then flicking it lightly from side to side. Now and then he pushed his tongue into her, using it like a tiny cock to rim her vaginal entrance. Marika opened her legs wider and sank down onto his face.

Juan made little noises of pleasure as her hot fragrant flesh covered his mouth and nose. It seemed as if he could not get enough of her. Her sex seemed to flutter and swell as he mouthed the tender flesh. His lips ground against her in an erotic kiss and Marika was carried along on the tide of slippery, tingling, exquisite pleasure.

Then she was coming, the orgasm bursting within her like a dam overflowing. She rubbed herself on Juan, using him solely as an instrument to satisfy herself, knowing that he loved her most un-English lack of control.

She meshed her fingers in his hair, pulling it free of its thong. 'Oh, yes. God, yes,' she groaned as his silky hair spilled around her fingers and the sweetly throbbing pleasure rioted through her.

For a moment longer, Juan held her hips. He pressed kisses to her mound, belly, and upper thighs, whispering endearments in his own language. Marika was still catching her breath when he pulled away and looked up at her face.

'And now. My reward?' he said, clasping his hand around his cock which looked ready to burst. 'I shall fuck you so well, beautiful lady.'

Marika shook her head almost regretfully as she let her skirt drop down to cover her legs. He was so tempting with his flushed face and loose dark hair.

'Your reward,' she said, 'is that you can make yourself come. And I shall watch you.'

'But no, I – I cannot . . . Not in front of you,' Juan stammered, but she saw that the prospect excited him further.

Already his hand was working faster, stroking and pumping his shaft. His hips began moving and his strong, sportsman's thighs flexed and relaxed. One hand moved up to caress his broad chest as he continued to stroke his cock, squeezing the engorged wet glans and capturing the drops of lubricant with his palm.

He chewed at his bottom lip and a groan escaped him. Juan ran his free hand over his bulging pectorals, dragging his fingertips across the tiny peaks of his erect nipples. She saw that his pubic hair grew up in a point towards his navel and his belly was ridged with muscle.

He was a beautiful male animal and she felt herself growing excited again as she watched him perform at her bidding. It would not be long now, she thought. Even as she watched closely Juan's face contorted and his thighs tensed.

'Ah, ah . . .' he grunted, his mouth sagging open as spurts of creamy liquid jetted from him.

For a moment he remained hunched over, the after-shocks of pleasure chasing across his face, then he took out a handkerchief and wiped himself clean. Slowly he rose to his feet and held out a hand to Marika. She slipped her hand into his and he brought it to his lips. Quietly and with something approaching humility, he said, 'No one ever treated me like that before. You are an extraordinary woman. Would you do me the honour of walking with me in the maze?'

Marika smiled. 'I'd be delighted, Juan. Besides I think we have much to talk about. Tell me, you said, did you not, that Charles is involved with this society of yours?'

Chapter Four

THE INTERIOR OF the Château blazed with the light of thousands of candles. Splinters of crystal reflecting from the cut glass of the many mirrors and chandeliers gave the atmosphere a fairy tale quality.

Marika descended the marble staircase with care, holding up the sumptuous folds of her gown with both hands. She felt more than a little self-conscious in the revealing costume and was glad of the ornate bird mask which hid the upper part of her face.

On returning to her room after the garden party she had found a large box containing her costume on her bed. With it were explicit instructions. She was told to wait until the servant arrived to dress her hair and help with her preparations for the ball. The dress with its back lacing would have been impossible to put on alone.

The heat rose in her cheeks as she recalled the deft hands of the handsome young man who had insisted on bathing her, powdering her all over with silvery dust, dressing her hair, and making up her face. His touch had been at once skilful and dispassionate. It had been a real luxury to have the handsome young servant to wait on her every whim and she felt mildly ashamed that she had responded physically to his professional ministrations.

Though he had given no sign of the fact, she felt sure that he knew how pleasant she had found his touch. It had been tempting to relieve herself of the sexual tension, but she had desisted from doing so. Now she was conscious of the feeling of latent sexual excitement simmering away just below the surface of her skin.

The masked ball was to be the highlight of the festivities and she did not quite know what to expect. Although she resisted at first, she could not help scanning the immediate area for any sign of Charles. Lord, what would he say when he saw what she was wearing?

Reaching the foot of the stairs, she walked across the marble tiles and down the corridor which led to the ballroom. The wire-frame of the skirt swayed gently as she walked and the movement of sheer black silk against her naked skin was like a lover's caress. She held her back straight so that her naked breasts, pushed up and out by the see-through, black lace corset, were shown to advantage.

As she neared the ballroom, she saw that every wall had been hung with luscious swags of black gauze, sewn with sequins and stars. Garlands of flowers and leaves, all dyed black and silver, were draped over doorways and looped around the window frames.

Marika was enchanted by the transformation of the glittering golden ballroom into a mysterious shadowy grotto. By some magic there was a haze of smoke in the room and she could see the fantastic shapes of feathered headdresses, spreading skirts, and pale limbs moving to and fro through the wispy, gun-metal strands.

A figure stepped forward and resolved itself into a man. Charles? She could not tell at first. He was tall enough and he held himself like Charles did, but this man wore a bird mask of black feathers. Ah, there was the tell-tale glint of his grey hair.

Charles came and stood beside her, holding out his arm so that she could rest her hand on it. It seemed that he wanted to keep up the pretence of anonymity. Her lips twitched. Why not? As he led her into the ballroom, he turned towards her and said, 'May I say that you look absolutely stunning.'

Marika flicked open the black fan which hung at her wrist and brought it up to cover her mouth.

'Why thank you, sir,' she said, executing a graceful curtsy.

She was grateful once more for the mask covering her face. She felt herself blushing as Charles's glance swept down to her nipped-in waist and then back up to fasten on her exposed breasts. The globes of creamy skin were speckled with silver glitter and the manservant had insisted on circling her nipples with silver paint.

'I very much approve of that effect,' Charles said. 'The black and silver with your fair hair is stunning. You're like the Snow Queen and the Queen of the Night rolled into one.'

She smiled, recalling the story of the Snow Queen.

'Aren't you afraid that I'll set a chip of ice in your heart and bind you to me forever?'

Charles shook his head and said seriously, 'I'm no young Kay, to be enchanted by your magic. But I am very smitten by you and I do have plans for us.'

Marika had spoken lightly and was astonished by the emotion in his voice. But, before she could respond, he led her into the throng of guests and she found herself staring at all the fabulous costumes. There was a profusion of chiffon, silks, velvets, all looped up over wide wire frames. She noticed that many of the women were bare-breasted and their legs and buttocks gleamed palely through their wide skirts. All of them wore masks, topped by feather headdresses, sewn with jewels and sequins.

'Champagne?' Charles said, taking two glasses from a silver tray.

Marika sipped, looking at him from under her lashes. His costume of black-satin frock coat and velvet breeches fitted him perfectly. Black riding boots reached to his knees.

'Did you have a pleasant afternoon?' she asked him dryly.

He chuckled. 'I did indeed. And so, it seems, did you. Juan told me about what happened in the maze. Quite forceful aren't you, when you want to be?'

'The situation seemed to demand it,' she said. 'Juan is spoiled and brash.'

'Quite so. He needed training. I approve absolutely.'

'Do you?' she said, before she could hide her surprise. Then she shrugged. 'Well, I'm sure that your opinion makes no difference to me, either way.'

'I hope that's not true,' Charles said gallantly.

Does he know that I'm lying, she thought. His opinion was suddenly of paramount importance to her. She was delighted that he found her beautiful and desirable. Her nipples had hardened until they resembled two silver beads. She was horribly aware of her exposed legs and buttocks and the fact that, when the sheer folds of the dress swayed apart – which they did with her slightest movement – Charles could see the silver-dusted hair of her pubic mound.

'Would you like to dance?' Charles asked, taking away her champagne and setting it down on a side table before she could protest.

He led her on to the dance floor, where other couples were moving gently to the classical strains of a string quartet.

'I'm not very good at this sort of dancing,' Marika said. 'I haven't had much practice. Nightclub discos are more my style.'

Charles pulled a face. 'We're in the eighteenth

41

century tonight. Don't shatter the illusion. Just relax and follow me. Do you like Mozart?'

Marika did. Although she was not knowledgeable about classical music, she could tell that this arrangement was a perfect choice for the ball. Charles was a superb dancer. She found that she was enjoying herself immensely. His arms around her were strong, almost protective but somehow managing to impose a sort of restraint on her. His smell, woody cologne and clean maleness was exciting. As they glided around the floor, she leaned in to him and felt the hard column of his body pressing against the whole length of her semi-nakedness.

What was it about this man that was so compelling?

'Won't your friends be missing you?' she asked when they stopped to drink their champagne.

He smiled in that way he had that made her feel uneasy. And she thought of all the things Juan had told her that afternoon – how Charles had formed his own secret society after being thrown out of the Discipline of Pearls for bad conduct, whatever that was. She suspected that Charles was ruthless and dangerous and she really ought not to be encouraging him in any way. But his reputation for trouble intrigued her. What could he have done that was so terrible?

'Greta and Juan, missing me? I think not,' Charles said, looking at her closely. 'What are you thinking? You look distracted.'

She raised her chin and looked directly at him. His light blue eyes glittered through the holes in his mask. For a moment she was reminded of another man, someone else who had a reputation for being manipulative and reckless and going his own way.

Stone.

The man she could love if he allowed her to. A shiver trailed down her spine. Did she really need another man like Stone in her life?

Charles was still waiting for an answer. 'I . . . I was thinking that I should not monopolise you any longer,' she said, beginning to draw away. 'Thank you for the dance, but I think I should circulate. I've hardly spoken to the other guests and I ought to be sizing up the competition for tomorrow.'

Charles closed an iron hand on her wrist.

'Don't be absurd. Do you think I'd let you go off to indulge in small talk? That's a poor excuse for leaving the most interesting man in the room.' He grinned and she could not help but respond, although her lips trembled when she smiled. 'You need not fear me, Marika. At least, only enough so that things are interesting. I want you, it's true. But I also want the same things as you do. Remember? The pursuit of pleasure is everything. There is nothing else worth striving for. I thought we agreed on that point.'

'I didn't agree to anything. You talked and I listened.'

Charles seemed to lose patience. 'You still need convincing? Come with me.'

He took a step and pulled her after him, so that she stumbled on her trailing skirt. Her temper rose at this cavalier treatment. She was not going to be dragged around like a rag doll.

'Take your hands off me,' she said. 'You think you can just snap your fingers and I'll do whatever you want? Well you're wrong. I'm staying right here. I want some more champagne and then I'd like to dance again.'

'I don't think so,' Charles said, unmoved by her show of spirit. 'Do you want me to drag you across the floor? I'm quite capable of doing so. No one will stop me. They'll think that it's all part of the festivities. If you don't believe me, look around.'

Marika turned her head and saw that Charles was right. The music had changed, taking on a wild rakish

43

note. The dancing had become more frenzied and a group of people were standing in a circle clapping, while a man slowly stripped the clothes from a woman wearing a red cat mask. The woman cupped her breasts, holding them out like offerings to the laughing guests. Her nipples were as bright and shiny as glacé cherries and the patch of hair between her sturdy thighs was coloured flame red.

Marika looked away. Through the drifting smoke she could see a woman in a spotted white gown, sitting astride a man on all fours. The dress was all rucked up around her waist and her bare buttocks bobbed up and down as her 'mount' scuttled around the floor. She was crying, 'Tally Ho!' and striking the taut cloth of the man's breeches with her folded fan.

'Satisfied?' Charles said, beginning to stride towards the ballroom door. 'No one will turn a hair, whatever we do. I suggest that you gather up your skirts, otherwise you'll take a tumble. Though I must confess the prospect of your bottom and pretty legs all laid bare and waving around in a froth of skirts is very pleasing.'

Marika fumed, but could do nothing to stop Charles dragging her into a corridor. She knew already how strong he was and decided to go along with whatever plan he had in mind. As soon as he let his guard down she would make her escape. Holding her skirts high she hurried to keep up with him, her heels clicking and sliding on the marble floor.

In a few moments Charles stopped suddenly and she almost crashed into him. They had not gone far. She could still hear the sound of music and revelry from the ballroom. Charles twitched a tapestry aside to reveal a stretch of panelling. He pressed a concealed switch and a length of the panelling swung inwards. Making a motion for her to be quiet Charles stepped through the opening and pulled Marika in after him.

'What's going on—' she began, but got no further as Charles clamped a hand over her mouth.

'I told you to be silent,' he hissed. 'Do you wish them to know we are here? Relax and enjoy the spectacle.'

Let *who* know we are here? she thought, feeling around in the dark space and finding that it was just big enough to hold a large sofa. There were holes in the wall in front of her and light streamed into the alcove from a room beyond.

Charles sat down and pulled her down beside him. The eye holes were positioned so that anyone seated could spy on the occupants of the other room. Charles motioned for her to look.

Reluctantly Marika leaned forward. What she saw set the erotic tension curling in her belly. There was a man and woman in the room. The woman was bent over a table, her glittery, red chiffon skirts were folded above her waist. Her bottom, which was quite large and firm, looked pale above the top of her red lace hold-up stockings.

It was not possible to see the woman's face as it was pressed to the table, but Marika recognised something about the woman's demeanour and the tumble of dark hair. It was Greta, and the man who stood at her side, stroking the pale globes of her buttocks with an air of contemplation, was Juan. Then Marika saw what she had missed at first. Greta's bottom was not uniformly pale. Thin red lines bisected the firm skin.

Marika almost gasped with shock. Greta had been beaten and those were recent marks. She looked at Charles. His face was only just visible in the gloom.

'You did that to her. This afternoon.' It was not a question.

Charles smiled, but did not deny it. 'Why look so surprised? You understand the necessity for training. Surely you are not jealous, my dear?'

'I won't dignify that with an answer.'

45

Marika chewed at her bottom lip. His arrogance was infuriating, but he was no spoilt child – unlike Juan. Juan had been easy to manage; she had met many men like him, but Charles was different, unfathomable. Everything Charles did seemed calculated. He burned coldly, like iron in winter. She ought to shout and scream and fight her way out of the cubicle, but she didn't because the man and woman in the other room were moving and she could not take her eyes from them.

Juan began spanking Greta's bottom while she writhed and moaned.

'Ah, you like?' he murmured. 'Charles has made you hot for me, no?'

'Yes. Oh, yes.' Greta arched her back, pushing her bottom towards Juan, eager for the next slap. 'Do it to me, Juan. Please.'

'Soon, my love,' Juan said huskily and continued spanking her. 'I'll pleasure you when I am ready. I want to feel your hot flesh against my belly as I thrust my *palo* into you.'

Greta moaned and tossed her head from side to side. It was obvious to Marika that the woman was not in pain. Rather she was highly excited. The blows were not hard, but soon Greta's bottom turned a uniform pink and the marks of her earlier beating became less visible. Juan paused and stroked Greta's bottom as if assessing the degree of warmth.

Satisfied, Juan opened his breeches and took out his cock. It sprang free, already erect. Leaning forward, he placed his shaft lengthways in the crease of Greta's buttocks. His eyes closed and it seemed to Marika that he was allowing the heat of Greta's bottom to sink into his cock.

Greta wriggled under her lover, pressing herself back against him, lifting her bottom so that her cheeks opened and the tender inner surfaces rubbed against his shaft. As the tip of Juan's cock emerged from Greta's crease, Marika could see that the moist reddish glans was entirely free of the cock-skin.

'Now. Do it now, Juan,' Greta whimpered, parting her thighs invitingly.

'You give me an order! Have you learned nothing?' Juan rapped, pulling backwards, so that his member sprang up between them.

He slapped her bottom, hard. The sound of it was loud in the room. Greta cried out with mingled pain and delight. Juan spanked her again.

'You are too eager,' he admonished. 'Remember what you have been taught. Obedience is all. What have you to say?'

'I'm sorry,' Greta said, between clenched teeth. 'Please forgive me. I'll be good this time. I promise.'

Juan took hold of her wrists and held them together in the small of her back. With his other hand he reached under her body and slid two fingers straight into her vagina. Greta sighed and moaned as Juan moved his fingers in and out of her. She worked her hips shamelessly, rubbing the sodden flesh of her sex against his hand.

Marika felt a dart of desire penetrate deeply into her belly. Flashes from her own past played across her mind. She knew how it felt to be spanked, to experience the tingling soreness of hot flesh coupled with the sensations of raging desire. It was a heady mix and she understood why Greta was enjoying playing the part of the submissive. How intriguing it was too, to see Juan in this new role after his performance in the maze that afternoon.

'Enjoying this?' Charles bent close to whisper, his hot breath tickling her ear.

Marika did not trust herself to reply. She was jerked back to the present by Charles's proximity and recalled the feel of his knowing fingers on her, in her. The way he had smoothed her sex-flesh, rubbed her aching and pinching bud, eased her wet folds apart . . . Oh, God. She could not stop trembling.

'Please. I beg you. Grant me release,' Greta whispered.

It could have been an echo of Marika's thoughts in her bedroom on that first night in the Château.

For a while longer Juan stroked Greta's sex, holding open her slippery folds and pushing his fingers deeply into her. Marika could see the reddish-brown lips of Greta's intimate flesh. The black hair on her mons was glistening with pearly juices.

Marika fidgeted on the sofa, imagining what the other woman must be feeling and aware of the swollen wetness of her own sex. She seemed to be sitting in a hot well of arousal and she knew, absolutely, that Charles was perfectly aware of that fact.

Greta's bottom quivered and her legs scissored wildly. She writhed and moaned, convulsing around Juan's hand. She must have had at least two climaxes, Marika thought, even before Juan decided to pleasure her with his cock. When Juan did finally sink himself into her, Greta began bucking up and down, grunting incoherently as he rode her hard.

Marika pressed her knuckles against her mouth. The two people in the next room were unaware of anything besides themselves and for a moment, she had been almost as involved in the scenario as they were.

It was a shock to feel Charles's hand on her arm and to be reminded of how strong he was as he drew her effortlessly towards him.

'Come here,' he said. 'You've seen enough. I want to find out for myself if you are as pliant and willing as Greta or whether you're going to need training, as she did.'

Marika was too aroused to resist him or to register the fact that he was talking about some imaginary future which included herself. Her body felt boneless, her senses stirred to a fever pitch of wanting. When he tipped her face up to his, she surrendered to the firm hardness of his lips on hers.

He kissed her expertly, his tongue thrusting strongly into her mouth, tasting, exploring, possessing. She gave herself willingly, tasting him in return and allowing the tactile onslaught. Then his lips were on her neck and she gave a tiny shiver as he bit down gently. The nipping at her skin was so nearly painful, yet so tantalising, that she gasped.

Charles laughed, deep in his throat, as his lips travelled lower and captured her nipple. Marika surged against him, feeling the wonderful, tingly pulling as his lips worried the hard little peak. There seemed to be a thread, directly connecting her breasts with her sex, for whenever a man suckled her she felt the pleasure reflected in the hot swollen flesh between her thighs.

Charles laid her on the couch, face down. She struggled a little, wishing to lie face to face – she wanted to be joined with him at both mouth and sex – but he held her down easily.

'This is what *I* want. Behave. Must I spank you too?' he murmured.

'Don't you dare!' she hissed back.

The thought was too awful, too shaming, but it was a beguiling prospect all the same. The couple in the other room could surely hear everything, as she could hear their cries and moans and the kiss of flesh meeting flesh. A new level of excitement blossomed within her. She felt her clit pulsing and more of the creamy wetness slid out of her vagina. Then Charles lifted her so that she was bent over the arm of the sofa. He threw her skirts over her head and covered her, crushing the flimsy wire frame between their bodies.

There was a moment's pause, when he put on a

condom, and then he slid straight into her. Marika tensed as his cock filled her, pressing right up under her pubic bone and butting against her womb. The intense pleasure she felt at being taken so forcefully frightened her.

She whispered urgently to Charles, 'Go slowly.'

He took no notice, plunging into her, digging his fingers into her buttocks and pulling them apart so that he could pound against the firm flesh.

Even though he took his pleasure selfishly, she matched him stroke for stroke. This is what she had wanted, since first he stepped into her room – was it only last night? His cock nudged against her inner walls and she slammed back onto him, feeling her juices lubricating, soaking his invasive, selfish cock.

But you can't just *take* me, it's not that simple, she thought. Men always think that they are the 'doers' and therefore ultimately dominant. But I'm *taking* you too. I'm enfolding you, imprinting you with my female scent and the texture of my most secret flesh. You won't forget me quickly, Charles Germain, I promise you, she exulted.

Her vagina convulsed around him as she came, the ridged walls squeezing and milking him. He still thrust into her as she orgasmed, riding her sensitised pulsing flesh.

'God. My God . . . Charles . . . darling . . .' she cried.

With a groan Charles came too, his face buried against her neck, his lips nuzzling her hair. She felt his every muscle tense as he spilled himself into her. His fingers were like claws on her buttocks, digging into the inner surfaces, dragging her open until her anus pouted like a tiny willing mouth. She bit her lip, wincing at the pinching soreness, even while she welcomed the evidence of his loss of control.

Then it was over. He withdrew quickly and moved away.

'Don't ever call me that,' he said, his face set and serious.

'What? What did I call you?' she said.

'Darling,' he said. Then he grinned wickedly. 'But God's all right.'

Marika could not help but laugh. Charles had seemed so dangerous and his influence on Juan and Greta was almost sinister. But his sense of humour endeared him to her. While she shook out her crushed skirts and tried to rearrange her feathered mask, which had been squashed underneath them, she wondered if she had not misjudged him.

But she knew deep down that she was not wrong about him. Her instincts were sound. It was one thing to share an erotic encounter with Charles Germain, but quite another to even *think* about trusting him.

Marika sat with the other guests in the Château's magnificent long gallery. Sunshine streamed in through domed skylights set at intervals in the vaulted ceiling. The light picked out accents on the gilded wall panels and made the colours of the tapestries as bright as stained glass.

The auction had been in progress for some time. As each book or print was sold, she jotted down the sale price in the margin of the catalogue, sure that the Major would find the figures of interest on her return.

She knew that outwardly she appeared calm, but inside she was aware of a mounting unease. Each item from the collection so far had fetched a price far in advance of anything she had anticipated. She desperately wanted to be successful on her first assignment, but she was beginning to have her doubts as to whether she could compete with the other guests at this level. Some extremely wealthy individuals were gathered together on the Ronsard estate.

At the back of the room the Japanese man and the man whom Charles had mentioned in connection with an oil magnate, were on the telephone to their clients. Between them the two men had bought most of the items. The Japanese man inclined his head as the auctioneer asked him if he wished to raise his bid. A few moments later the gavel fell and another item had been bought.

There were only a few lots to go before Marika must join the bidding. She glanced at Charles, who sat a few seats away to her left. He smiled at her, perfectly composed and looking immaculate in a dark suit.

Swallowing her anxiety Marika concentrated on the auction. The first item she wanted was the original manuscript of a little-known novel by Leopold von Sacher-Masoch. The bidding began. Trying not to be overwhelmed by the starting price, Marika held back for a while before joining the bidding. Already the bids had far exceeded the reserve price and, as no let seemed imminent, she began to seriously doubt whether she could secure the manuscript.

Soon there were only three people left in the bidding. The Japanese man, Charles Germain, and herself. The auctioneer looked rapidly from one to the other. Marika felt her spirits sinking as Charles glanced triumphantly at her and named a figure she could not hope to match. There was a collective gasp. Marika shook her head, the Japanese man conferred with his client then made a negative gesture with one hand. The gavel fell.

'Sold to the gentleman,' the auctioneer said.

Marika crossed her legs and clenched her hands in her lap, not caring that she crumpled the slubbed silk of her emerald skirt.

Charles had out-bid her on purpose. He knew that she was desperate to obtain the Sacher-Masoch. She fumed inwardly, but there was no time to dwell on her anger and disappointment as the other items she had marked were being held up to view.

'A first edition De Sade. Pristine condition. Who'll start me at one thousand?' the auctioneer began. 'You sir? One thousand I'm bid. Do I hear fifteen hundred? Two thousand I'm bid . . .'

Marika steeled herself to stay calm. She was confident that she could out-bid everyone for the De Sade. Now that the Sacher-Masoch had gone she had extra money to spend on the other items on the list. The bids came in fast and Marika kept pace at first. But soon the figure began approaching the upper limit of her means. She went over her top price, but then dropped out of the bidding.

'Twenty thousand. Any more bids? I'm selling . . . Once. Twice . . .'

Charles named a figure far in excess of the last bid. There were no other bids. Marika knew that she must conserve the remainder of her funds for the items of lesser interest. She was too stunned to react as she heard the sound of wood striking and the De Sade also went to Charles. A ripple of applause accompanied the successful sale. There were whispers of congratulation nearby.

Marika sat woodenly, plucking at the corner of her catalogue. The bastard. The absolute bastard. Tears of anger pricked her eyes. The two items she had wanted most of all were lost to her. She had so wanted to prove to the Major that she was equal to the task of acting as his agent. She wished that she had never laid eyes on Charles Germain.

The rest of the auction passed in a blur. Most of the rarer books and prints had been sold now and Marika was able to secure the rest of the items on her list with little difficulty.

She did not see Charles as she went to claim her purchases after the sale. Which was a good thing. She felt murderous towards him. After paying for the items, she took the pile of books directly to her room.

Wrapping each item carefully in bubble packing, she packed them in a box. Lunch had been set out for the guests in the dining room, but Marika decided to pack her case and leave at once. There seemed no point in lingering. She had what she had come for. And she could not bear to see the self-satisfied expression on Charles's face.

Had he been playing with her all along? She found it difficult to believe that he had simply amused himself at her expense, while all the time he had been planning to humiliate her at the auction. She knew that he had enjoyed the sex as much as she had, but she knew also that many men, women too, were able to divorce pleasure from business. Hadn't she been able to do that in certain circumstances herself?

Charles Germain was on a power trip. He had to be in control, whether it was sex or money, or she suspected, anything else in his life. The enforcement of one will over another. That was the sum total of his interest. She knew that now.

What an idiot I am, she told herself, I ought to have seen this coming. Back in London she was going to have some explaining to do and she was not looking forward to that. Humble pie had a bitter taste.

As she was fastening her case, there was a knock on her door. She opened it distractedly, still thinking of the Major and how disappointed he would be.

'You!' she said as Charles stepped into the room. 'I didn't think you'd show your face. If you've come here to gloat, don't bother. I've nothing to say to you. Why don't you just go?'

Charles had changed into a cream polo shirt and grey cords. In one hand he carried a briefcase. Eyeing her packed case, he asked, 'Leaving already? There's gratitude for you. I'm surprised, Marika. I didn't imagine that you'd slink off without speaking to me. Surely cowardice isn't your style?'

Angry words rose in her throat, but she didn't voice them, uncomfortably aware that he was right. She was running away, cutting her losses and getting out with the shreds of her pride intact. She glared at him.

'What do you mean "gratitude"?'

He smiled, his light blue eyes flashing with humour.

'But I thought you knew. I told you that you'd need my help to get the items you wanted. Surely you remember? We spoke about it during the viewing. Well I bought them for you, but it seems that you are questioning my motives.'

She was confused. Was it possible that she had misjudged him?

'Do you mean that you are willing to sell them to me at a loss?'

'Of course. I know how badly you wanted them.'

Marika was stunned. There had to be more to this. She was certain that Charles was not the sort of man who went in for charity. He knew what she could afford to pay him and it was far short of what he had paid. He stood to lose thousands of pounds if he handed the books over.

'What's in this for you?' she asked dryly. 'I can't see you in a white beard and red robes, sitting on a sleigh.'

He grinned. 'Ah, that's better. I prefer you when you're on the attack. I'll hand the book and manuscript over with pleasure. The money means nothing to me. But I want your promise that you'll make yourself available to me in London for certain assignments.'

'What assignments?'

'You'll have to wait and see. Come on, Marika, where's your sense of adventure? You've covered this ground before. It'll be no different to the sort of thing you've done in the name of the Discipline of Pearls.'

Marika considered his offer. It was true that she had,

in the past, been sent on certain assignments. Usually a black card with a phone number in gold lettering would drop through her letter-box. Always there was the element of choice. No one ever pressured her to do anything she did not want to. With Charles, she suspected that choice would not be high up on his personal agenda.

'Why were you thrown out of the Discipline of Pearls?' she said.

Charles's face darkened. 'You know about that? Of course. Juan has been talking. Let's just say that some of my activities attracted disapproval. I was asked, politely, to leave. So I set up a splinter group, where my particular tastes are catered for. If you want to know more, you must accept my invitation.'

Marika was curious, but every instinct was screaming at her not to get involved with Charles. The attraction between them was too strong. It would not take much for it to burst into flame and she felt that one or both of them might be consumed by the heat.

Quickly, she weighed things up. It was important to her that she acquire the manuscript and book and Charles was more than willing to sell them to her. That meant that she could return to the Major in triumph. Everything else was part of a possible future. In London things were different. She could avoid Charles, not return his calls, and he would ultimately lose interest.

'I accept your terms,' she said.

He smiled triumphantly and put the briefcase on her bed. Snapping open the locks, he said, 'I knew you would. You cannot resist a challenge, can you?'

Marika returned his smile. That much was true. It was the reason why she had allowed herself to be recruited into the Discipline of Pearls in the first place. The society was mysterious and compelling, all the more so for functioning within a set of strict rules.

Charles Germain was the sort of man who made up his own rules and the society she respected had thrown him out. Just what had she let herself in for?

'You realise that our agreement is binding?' Charles said. 'Word of mouth is as good as a contract to me.'

Marika nodded, already wondering if she had been too hasty. Perhaps she ought to change her mind. She kept silent. A promise exchanged under duress wasn't binding after all. It was the same as crossing your fingers.

Charles leaned forward and kissed her on the mouth. It was a firm kiss, almost without passion.

As she returned the pressure of his lips, it felt to Marika as if she gave Charles a Judas kiss. But, she told herself, he would never know.

Chapter Five

MARIKA NOSED HER BMW through the familiar London streets, heading towards Hampstead. She had returned from the Loire Valley only the day before, but it already seemed as if the Ronsard Château, Charles Germain, and the auction had all been part of some waking dream.

She slid her hand around the steering wheel as she negotiated a turning, enjoying the feeling of leather against her palm. The afternoon sun was low enough in the sky to dazzle her and she slipped on a pair of Ray-Bans. On the seat beside her was the case containing her carefully wrapped purchases. She could hardly wait to see the delight on the Major's face when she handed them over to him.

She parked the car in front of the detached Victorian house, then walked up the tiled path to the ornate porch which framed the front door.

'Hello, Beth,' she said as the maid let her into the house and showed her straight through to the library.

'Nice to see you again, Madame. Did you have a good trip?' Beth asked.

'Yes, thank you. Very successful.'

Marika liked the efficient young woman who acted as nurse-companion, as well as performing light duties around the house. Beth wore the pendant which signified that she was a member of the secret society and no doubt counted it a privilege to perform other more intimate services for the Major.

Marika found the Major sitting in a studded red leather chair, a book on his lap. The fire in the grate looked cheerful and welcoming. The room smelt of lavender polish and leather. She went to stand beside his chair.

'Marika, my dear. It's always such a pleasure to see you.'

She kissed his cheek. 'I'm pleased to be back.'

It was true, she realised. This room with its walls lined with bookshelves, its antique mahogany furniture and dark red walls, had become a home from home.

The Major's thick white hair was brushed back from his forehead. He looked like a country landowner in his mustard, crew-necked sweater and tweeds.

'Sit down opposite me,' he said warmly. 'I want to hear about everything that happened over the weekend. You look lovely as usual. Did you leave behind any broken hearts in France?'

She smiled at his teasing tone, as his eyes swept over her neat figure in the short, cherry-red Gucci suit. She always took pains with her appearance when visiting him, knowing how much he appreciated the good things in life. Once the Major had been a strong and vital man, a lover of many beautiful women, but age had added a yellow tinge to his skin and turned his eyes to the colour of stone-washed denim.

Because of his failing health he rarely left the house and visits from society members were scarce.

'Broken hearts? Only one or two,' she said, smiling fondly at him.

He grinned, the humour enlivening his face and disguising the hollows of his cheeks.

'Ah. So few? But I trust that you enjoyed yourself. I shall want to hear all about that too. In detail as usual, but first, coffee?'

Marika nodded. 'Please.'

She was looking forward to telling him about her erotic experiences. He was probably the one man in the world who she could speak to about anything and everything. Although the Major occupied an illustrious position within the Discipline of Pearls, their relationship had rapidly become similar to that of father and daughter.

While the Major rang for the housekeeper, Marika picked up the case which she had set on the floor next to her chair and laid it on her lap. Taking out the first carefully wrapped package, she pulled open the bubble packing and held the manuscript out to him. The Major's faded blue eyes quickened with interest.

'The Sacher-Masoch? My dear, but that's absolutely wonderful!' He took the bound sheaves from her, running trembling hands over the sheets of yellowing paper. 'It's magnificent. Priceless . . .' he murmured.

He beamed at Marika. 'I thought I could rely on you and now I see that I need not have had the slightest doubt as to your abilities. Is that the De Sade too? Splendid! I'm quite overwhelmed. Did you have any trouble getting these two? I was worried that the competition might be fierce. There are more people than ever collecting erotica these days.'

'No problems at all,' Marika lied. 'I found the auction exciting. It was quite a challenge too.'

She had considered confiding in the Major about Charles, but on reflection had decided not to mention him. There was probably no need to worry. She did not anticipate seeing the man ever again.

'You've done an excellent job. I think a generous bonus is in order.' He named an amount and Marika made a sound of protest. He held up his hand. 'No.

60

No. Don't attempt to refuse. I absolutely insist. You're far too modest.'

Marika felt a mild twinge of guilt, but shook it off immediately. The coffee arrived and Marika helped herself to a cup while the Major examined all the items she had purchased, turning over pages and stroking the cloth and leather bindings.

Later, she accepted the Major's invitation to stay to dinner. The food was excellent as usual, imaginative but traditional English fare which was the Major's preference. It was not until they were sipping after-dinner liqueurs, that Marika brought up the subject which was often on her mind.

'Have you had any word from your nephew lately?'

The Major shook his head. 'Jordan's a busy man. I expect he'll visit me when he has time.'

Marika felt annoyed on the Major's behalf. Jordan Stone, the man who had introduced her to the secret society, ought to have the common decency to visit his uncle – the man who had virtually brought him up.

But, in the back of her mind, she knew that her anger with Stone was more personal. Why had he not contacted her in all these months? For she knew that their devastating encounter in Tuscany had meant as much to him as it had to her.

With the taste of her first success as the Major's agent still sweet in her mouth, Marika resumed her normal work timetable.

It was overcast as she drove to her PrimeLight office in the docklands. The colour of the sky matched the oily, battleship-grey of the Thames. The reflections of the modern linear buildings and the water-front warehouses were muted and sullen looking.

As soon as Marika sat down at her desk, Gwen breezed in bearing a tray of freshly made coffee.

'That's an ominous sign,' Marika said. 'I only get this treatment when you've something unpleasant to tell me.'

Gwen smiled. 'Not exactly unpleasant. It's just that Mr Danvers phoned. He'd like to speak to you again. Apparently he's not at all happy with the catalogue proofs.'

Marika groaned. 'Better tell the odious little man that I'll see him today. Do I have a window this afternoon?'

Gwen checked the appointment book. She nodded. 'Three-thirty?'

'Arrange that, will you? Thanks, Gwen. Right, I'd better go through this in-tray.'

The morning passed quickly. Marika gave her total attention to her work. Her expertise and dedication had made PrimeLight one of the premier PR companies in London. She had recently been made a director and was even more determined to give a good account of herself.

She was absorbed in reading the file on a long-term client when Gwen came into the office an hour later.

Gwen coughed theatrically and said with her usual dry humour, 'These just arrived for you. But I'll have them if you're not interested.'

Marika's eyes widened as she took in the enormous bouquet of creamy orchids. They were wrapped in french-blue foil and tied with a bow of black gauze. Reaching for the card Marika read, *I'll be in touch soon. Be ready. Charles.*

She felt a shiver of apprehension as she ran her thumb over the writing. It was spare, economical, stylish – like the man himself. Had she really imagined that she would be able to forget all about him on her return to London?

'Shall I put them in water?' Gwen said. 'Aren't they

beautiful. So striking. What do you think, the plain black Conran vase?'

'Oh, er . . . yes. Do whatever you like with them,' Marika said, dumping them into Gwen's outstretched arms, She really did not care whether Gwen stuffed them straight into a jam jar.

Gwen raised her eyebrows. 'What ingratitude. *I* should have such an admirer.'

Marika just smiled and ignored the question in Gwen's expression.

'The Conran vase it is then,' Gwen said, her lips twitching.

Marika worked on, trying to ignore the orchids which Gwen had placed on the deep window-sill behind her. They were just in her line of vision and she caught glimpses of them every time she turned her head. She had to admit that they *were* beautiful. It was being reminded of her obligation to Charles which she did not welcome. Finally she decided to see the orchids for what she hoped they were; just a gift from Charles, a token of his esteem. She refused to see anything more than that in the gesture.

At lunchtime she made her way to Canary Wharf, where she had arranged to meet a client. Westferry Circus was one of her favourite places. The public garden with its silver lime trees, lamps and benches was never crowded. At the far side of Cabot Square there was a glass-roofed building which housed the restaurant where she had booked a table.

She was a little early and ordered a white wine spritzer while she waited for Carol Oldston to arrive. Carol was a graduate of St Martin's School of Art, an award-winning jewellery designer, who wanted to cash in on her current high profile, before, as she put it, 'I become last week's news.'

Carol arrived promptly. She was an attractive twenty-five-year-old, bursting with enthusiasm, but willing to listen to Marika's ideas. The perfect client. Over a light salad lunch Marika discussed the different possibilities of publicising Carol's work. The meeting went well and she was satisfied that she had done the best for her client. After paying the bill, she gave Carol a folder containing a list of the proposals they had drawn up.

'I'm glad we're in agreement about the poster campaign. It's very cost effective for the effort involved,' Marika said. 'That and the exhibition, with magazine coverage, ought to bring you in a few commissions.'

She shook hands with Carol and they parted amicably. On her way back to the office, Marika sighed. Now why couldn't Danvers be as pleasant as that? She was not looking forward to her meeting with him.

It was after six when she left the office and headed for Primrose Hill. She was tired, irritated and looking forward to a soak in a hot bath. Danvers had been as obnoxious as she predicted. He seemed to have realised that she was immune to his clumsy, verbal advances and had decided to play the hard-nosed businessman.

Predictably the traffic queues were diabolical. She put a CD into the player and let the strains of Bryan Ferry's cover version of 'Smoke Gets in Your Eyes' wash over her. His evocative voice sent a chill down her spine. She smiled. Ferry was still the ace lounge lizard.

By the time she had bathed, changed into over-sized track pants and T-shirt and was sitting down to a plate of pasta it was past eight. She curled her feet underneath her and piled cushions at her back, preparing to have a TV dinner on the sofa.

Just as she was chewing the first mouthful, enjoying the taste of garlic and tomatoes, the phone rang.

Cursing under her breath, she put her plate aside and answered the phone.

'Marika? Guess who?'

'Pia? Is that you? How are you? Are you back in London?' Marika pushed her still-damp hair back from her face, her food and the TV film forgotten.

Pia laughed. 'So many questions! I'm in Rome. God, it's been so hectic lately. I'm doing a photo-spread for Italian *Vogue* this week, but I've a few days free at the end of the week. Can you meet me?'

'In Rome?'

'Yes. You could fly out on Friday at midday. Oh, say you will. I miss you, Marika. I can't stop thinking about Paris. I loved the time we spent there.'

Marika's stomach tightened. She pictured Pia's face, her perfect olive skin, tilted dark eyes and her full red mouth. Just the mention of Paris had set her heart pounding. Pia had introduced her to the delights of loving a woman – something she would never have imagined possible, even in her wildest dreams.

But that was before she had become involved in the Discipline of Pearls and opened her mind to new pathways of pleasure.

'I miss you too, Pia,' she said softly. 'We never did take that break and get away to the Bahamas on your friend's yacht, did we?'

'No, we didn't. I'm sorry, Marika, but that's how it goes. In the modelling business it's hard to keep up friendships – even those that mean something special. You must be tired of getting hastily scribbled postcards from all around the globe. Come to Rome. Let me make it up to you.'

The huskiness and the hint of promise in Pia's voice played havoc with Marika's senses. She remembered the taste of the woman's mouth, the softness of her skin, her perfume. And the singular pleasure of stroking her intimate flesh and bringing her to orgasm.

65

Making love to Pia was like pleasuring an image of herself, intoxicating and somehow familiar.

Pia had been her partner in some of the most unpredictable encounters within the secret society. Hearing the model's voice made Marika realise that she missed receiving the black cards with the telephone numbers on them. The most exciting thing about phoning that number was that she never knew what to expect. She might be called upon to meet a society member in a hotel room, go to an address in Paris, or to attend a private function. The only rule was that, once the assignment was accepted, she was bound by total obedience.

'Am I breaking society rules again by contacting you direct?' Pia said, as if she had read Marika's thoughts. Her tone made it evident that she was unrepentant. 'I could have sent you one of those little black cards, but I'd heard that you'd risen too high now to be at the beck and call of any society member. I don't know that I envy you that. It's exciting sometimes to be *made* to perform for another person's pleasure.'

Marika laughed. 'You always were a risk-taker.'

'That's true. But it's more than just a cheap thrill with you. You know that. And you're a risk-taker too.'

Marika felt the truth of Pia's words. She felt herself wavering. She really ought not to indulge herself with another weekend away from her PrimeLight commitments. It was only last weekend that she had been at the Ronsard Château. But there was also the recollection of the last time she had seen Pia. It had been in Tuscany – with Stone. What had happened between them all in the back of the Mercedes had shaken her to the core.

What if Pia had news of Stone? What if she had seen him again, slept with him? A hot little dart of jealousy pierced her.

All these months and I'm still obsessed with the

man, she thought. The hand holding the phone had begun to tremble. She did not know whether the emotion she felt was for Pia or Stone. Closing her eyes briefly, she made a decision.

'All right. I'll come to Rome. Which hotel are you staying at?'

Pia told her, her voice rising on a note of excitement. 'See you soon then. Can't wait. I'll have the champagne on ice. Just wait until you see what I've got planned for us. You'll love it. Ciao.'

'Ciao,' Marika said and replaced the phone.

There was another reason why she was glad she was going to Rome. It would mean that Charles Germain would not be able to contact her for a few days.

It was raining as Marika climbed into the yellow taxi which was going to take her the eighteen miles from Fiumicino airport to the city of Rome.

The driver spoke perfect English and Marika gave him directions for Pia's hotel on the Via Veneto.

Wiping condensation from the glass, she peered through the rain-washed window as the taxi sped in the direction of the Via Aurelia. The hotel was a forty minute drive away. The previous night Pia had sent a fax, informing Marika that, should she arrive early, a message would be left for her at reception. She had also taken the liberty of informing the bookings manager that Marika would be a guest in her suite.

Soon they reached the centre of Rome, the taxi driver navigating the busy roads with expertise. They passed opulent stone buildings, fronted by magnificent marble steps. Stylish piazzas and modern theatres stood alongside each other in uneasy alliance. Marika noticed the Capuchin monastery which was famous for its subterranean chapels with their piled bones of some four thousand dead monks.

67

The lower reaches of Via Veneto slid sedately past the taxi window. At a busy intersection she saw the large white shape of the American Embassy. Pia's hotel, one of the most palatial in the area, was opposite. The taxi dropped her at the canopied foyer and the doorman carried her bags inside.

Marika's enquiry at the reception desk was greeted by a polite smile.

'Miss Fremen. Ah, yes. You are expected. I have a letter for you.' The desk clerk handed her a sealed envelope. 'You would like to go straight up to the suite, I think? Then Fabio here will show you where to go. I hope you enjoy your stay.'

Pia's suite was on the top floor of the hotel. Smooth, Empire-style fabrics and thick carpets in shades of gold and pale blue gave the place a plush but restful feel. A touch of luxury was provided by the crystal chandeliers, marble columns, and numerous arrangements of fresh flowers and fruit.

Marika thanked Fabio and tipped him, then closed the door as he left. Walking across the elegant lounge, she sat down on a pale blue sofa.

Sliding open the envelope, Marika began to read.

So sorry I shall miss your arrival, Pia wrote, *But we have had to re-shoot. There were problems yesterday, but I won't bore you with the details. Anyway, I've arranged a treat for you. It's very special. I can recommend it. Relax and enjoy it. I'll be back sometime this evening.*

Pia signed her name with a flourish. There was a line of crosses underneath.

Wondering what 'treat' Pia had arranged in her absence, Marika kicked off her shoes and padded into the larger of the two bedrooms. A canopied bed dominated the room. It was a confection of gilded cherubs, swathes of filmy blue and gold fabric, and an absolute profusion of satin-covered cushions. Why on earth would anyone need so many cushions? Marika thought. They came in all shapes, from small round ones to large, tube-shaped bolsters.

She was about to go into the bathroom to freshen-up before unpacking, when there was a knock at the door. She smiled to herself. This must be Pia's treat arriving.

'Miss Fremen?' the young man who stood there said.

'Yes,' Marika said, taking in the fact that the man was extremely good-looking.

He was holding a large leather case. Intrigued, she waited for him to present her with a gift. But instead, he made a polite movement and she realised that he wished to come into the room. Her innate sense of self-preservation made her stiffen slightly.

He seemed to sense her confusion and smiled disarmingly.

'Scuse. You are not expecting me? Then I explain. I am Giovanni. And I have been engaged to offer to you my professional services. I am fully trained personal attendant and masseur. You have me for two hours.'

Now she understood. How perceptive of Pia to think of something like this. Pia apparently had availed herself of Giovanni's singular talents. And no wonder. Giovanni was more than good-looking. He was drop-dead gorgeous.

'You come well recommended,' Marika smiled. 'You'd better come in.'

Giovanni walked over to a marble and glass table and laid his case down flat. He was not very tall, perhaps a little over five eight, but he was muscular and well proportioned. He smiled.

'We begin at once?'

'I . . . I was about to have a shower,' Marika said. 'I'll be ready in a moment. Help yourself to a drink.'

'Wait, please. I must explain,' Giovanni said. 'No shower. I do everything. I bathe you, wash your hair, perform a manicure, pedicure, everything you wish. I make you feel beautiful all over and then I make the massage with special oils. You will allow this, yes? I am the best. I will show you this.'

Film star looks and modest too, she thought. But who could resist such an invitation? Who would want to? The thought of being pampered from head to toe was wonderful, especially as she felt travel-worn and a little cramped from sitting around for most of the day.

'All right,' she said, then added with a touch of sarcasm, 'but I'll undress myself, if that's allowed.'

He grinned, showing the straightest, whitest teeth she had ever seen outside a toothpaste commercial. His dark eyes were fringed with long, sooty lashes. Rich brown hair, with a trace of curl brushed against the collar of his immaculate white jacket.

'Of course. I make you a cocktail while I wait. No, don't tell me how you like. Let me guess. It will be a challenge. I make a smooth cool drink for a beautiful, blonde English lady.'

God, he's just too perfect to be real, Marika thought as she closed the bathroom door. The fact that he was being paid to be so charming was far from her mind. Giovanni used his considerable presence to maintain the illusion that he was hers alone. At least for two hours.

She needed a moment to catch her breath. For a few seconds she stood with her back to the door, her palms pressed against the cool wood. This was as exciting as anything which had been arranged for her within the secret society.

She could hear Giovanni moving around the sitting room, opening doors, chopping things up, pouring ice into a glass.

Stripping off hastily, she dumped her clothes in the laundry tub provided, not caring that she crushed her expensive linen coat-dress. Her hair had been pinned into a French pleat. She pulled out pins and fluffed the pale strands over her shoulders before shrugging on Pia's silk kimono, which had been hanging on the bathroom door.

Giovanni glanced up as she emerged, his shapely mouth curving appreciatively.

'Please to sit down. Enjoy your drink. I have some preparations to make.'

She took the glass he held out. In the few minutes she had been in the bathroom he had worked a miracle. Was there no end to his talents? The long, frosted glass held a foamy concoction, the colour of palest, milky-green. Slices of fresh fruit decorated the rim.

While Giovanni disappeared into the bathroom, case in hand, Marika put her feet up on the sofa, lay back against the cushions and sipped. The icy tastes of coconut and limes, subtly spiked with alcohol fizzed in her mouth. It was wonderful. By the time Giovanni reappeared she had drained the glass and was feeling a touch light-headed.

'I am ready for you, *signorina*. Please to come this way.'

Marika stood up. Thanks Pia, she thought. I'm really going to enjoy this.

Chapter Six

THE BATHROOM HAD been transformed by drawn blinds and strategically placed candles. The room had a soft golden glow which lent the green marble walls and fittings a pearly luminescence.

'May I?' Giovanni asked softly, taking hold of the kimono and easing it down Marika's naked body.

He had stripped to the waist and wore only a pair of well-fitting white trousers. His muscular chest was smooth and golden, with only a sprinkling of dark hair between his pectorals. He indicated that she should get into the bath.

Perfumed steam rose from the surface of the water and Marika sighed as the heat caressed her skin. The bath was huge – a fat, oval-shaped pool, surrounded by a wide lip of marble. Set out all around were a profusion of lotions, shampoos and creams.

Marika lay back in the silky water and half-closed her eyes. The scent filling the room was delicious and she felt her knotted muscles beginning to relax. She anticipated the touch of Giovanni's expert hands, but was not prepared for what happened next.

Stepping out of his white trousers, Giovanni stood before her wearing only the scantiest of underwear. The snugly fitting tanga was hardly more than a posing pouch. It stretched tautly over the bulge at his groin.

'You're going to join me?' she said, amused by the fact that she felt slightly shocked. She really ought to be unshockable by now.

'But of course. How else am I to attend to your needs?'

There was a displacement of bath water as Giovanni climbed in beside her. Picking up a pad made of some kind of fibrous material, he poured a peach-coloured lotion into it. Marika gave herself up to total pleasure as he began to rub her limbs with the pad, moving it gently but firmly in a circular motion.

He covered every inch of her skin, manipulating her body efficiently and expertly, so that she did not need to do anything but lie back and enjoy it. The first treatment was designed simply for cleansing purposes, but as he replaced the pad with a soft sponge, she realised that his movements had become more sensual.

The sponge was soft on her freshly scrubbed skin, the creamy lather streaming over her bare shoulders and foaming down to cover her breasts. Her nipples hardened into prominent peaks and she felt a little self-conscious at how wanton they looked, peeping through the suds like reddish-brown cherries. Giovanni's fingers followed the trail of the sponge, stroking smoothly over her breasts and the slight mound of her belly. With the tip of one finger he circled her navel and finally dipped a hand between her thighs.

'I make you clean everywhere. I am very thorough, like doctor,' Giovanni said, as Marika failed to suppress a gasp.

His beautiful dark eyes glistened in the candle-light. A lock of damp hair fell forward onto his brow, casting a shadow on his golden skin. She felt herself responding in a purely animal way to his good looks and to his total dedication in giving her pleasure.

'Is good?' he asked softly, as his fingers continued their dance across her skin, smoothing more of the peach lather over the outer lips of her sex.

Oh Lord, he's thorough all right, she thought. Now he was cupping her buttocks, smoothing foam over the full globes. At the sureness of his touch and the subtle probing of his fingers as they went to work on her most intimate flesh, Marika let her legs fall open. If he was trying to arouse her, he was succeeding. But his whole attitude was one of cool professionalism. She was not sure whether there were limits to the 'special attentions' he had been paid for.

She lay back against the curved rim of the bath, her hair fanned out around her. The hot water lapped against her chin and the sexual tension began to build inside her. His fingers were slippery and gentle, pushing a little way inside her vagina and then sliding into her crease to circle her anus. If he did much more of that she was going to come.

Then Giovanni moved his hands back up to her breasts, squeezing them gently. He urged her to adjust her position.

'Sit now, please. Not too much pleasure. I make it last for you,' he said. 'I wash your hair now.'

Marika sat up and let her head fall back as Giovanni poured shampoo into her hair. Was it her imagination or had he sounded regretful when he took his hands away from between her legs? His professionalism seemed to be slipping. She decided to tease him a little.

With her back arched, her breasts jutted forward and her belly was pulled tight. She drew herself up, so that both breast and belly shape was exaggerated. She could almost feel his eyes on her, roving over the dips and hollows of her frame. Giovanni murmured a few words in Italian and she knew that he was finding the sight of her wet skin and well-toned body as arousing as she found his touch.

His fingers, strong but slender, kneaded her scalp, rubbing behind her ears and lingering on the two dips at the base of her skull. A trip to the hairdressers had never been like this. After conditioning, then rinsing her hair with the shower attachment, he combed the dripping strands back from her forehead.

She expected him to continue to wash her body and felt a pang of disappointment when he rinsed her skin and climbed out of the bath. Drying himself quickly, he held out a towelling robe for her. Marika patted her skin dry as Giovanni went into the bedroom. A short time later, her head swathed in a soft towel, she followed him.

Giovanni stood beside the marble-topped dressing table, naked except for the towel wrapped around his waist.

'Will you sit here, *signorina*?' he said, and when she did so, proceeded to blow-dry her hair into a mass of soft waves.

A manicure and pedicure were performed with the same speed and expert efficiency and then he asked her to lie on the bed.

Marika's pulses quickened. Giovanni must have been with her for over an hour already. She wished she had him for the whole afternoon. This was the part of the treatment she had been most looking forward to. A massage with scented oils was the ultimate luxury.

She shrugged off the towelling robe and sat on the cover which Giovanni had placed on the bed.

'On my stomach or my back?' she said, looking him straight in the eye.

She was pleased to see that he was discomforted by her nudity. In the bathroom she had been partially screened from his gaze by the milky bath water. The low lighting had added a note of modesty to the

75

proceedings, but here nothing was hidden from him.

She noticed how he stared at her breasts, particularly at her large dark nipples. His gaze flickered down to the shadowed mound between her legs. Not so unmoved now, are you? she thought. Giovanni was surely used to attending to beautiful women. She would have expected him to be somewhat immune to their charms. He was plainly not immune to hers. The towel at his waist had a definite bulge in it.

'Please to sit. I have another task to perform before I begin massage,' he said, his voice less steady than before.

He had a small tray in his hands and she saw that it contained a tiny pair of scissors, some damp tissues, and a little bottle of oil. Intrigued, she wondered what there could be left to do. She had already been primped from top to toe.

After placing a bolster-shaped cushion in the small of her back and asking her to lean against it, Giovanni knelt in front of her and put a hand on each thigh. Gently he pressed her legs open and lifted each foot, drawing it in towards her buttocks and placing the soles flat on the cover.

Marika's cheeks flamed. This was so unexpected. In this position the whole of her sex was opened and presented to his gaze. The fact that he was studying her damp pink folds with an interest that was decidedly unprofessional added to her discomfort. But she also felt a little flicker of triumph. The bulge in his towel was even more pronounced now.

'Oh,' she breathed, as he dipped into the tray, took hold of the scissors, and then ran the tips of his fingers through her pubic curls.

'I make you more beautiful here too,' he said. 'Don't worry. I am careful.'

By now, she was used to the feel of his hands on her and did not flinch as he began clipping away at the hair on her mons. He seemed to be concentrating on the strands that curled in towards her labia. He worked delicately, like an artist, cutting perhaps one or two hairs at a time.

He's thinning out the hair, so that more of my labia is exposed, she thought. Oh God, the pink tip of her clitoris would be visible if he cut away much more.

For some reason she found the thought unbearably exciting. Even with her legs closed, she would know that a tantalising glimpse of her moist slit remained on show. Giovanni's feather-light touch was as arousing as any direct stimulation. She began to squirm, knowing that he could sense her growing excitement and was pleased by it.

'Just a little longer,' he grinned. 'Turn over now.'

Oh, this was even worse. The cushion under her belly served to lift up her bottom and hips. When he parted her legs, her sex was presented like a split fruit and the open valley of her crease gave up its secrets readily. She felt the muscles around her anus contract with shame as Giovanni spread her even further apart with his fingers and began to snip away with his tiny scissors.

When he had finished her face was crimson and there was a familiar hot pulsing in her clitoris. He had not touched her sex directly, but she knew that her folds were swollen and her vagina was wet and receptive. When he had finished he asked her to sit up.

'You like?' Giovanni asked, holding a mirror for her to look into. 'Is beautiful, no?'

She looked down at herself. Only the sparsest frosting of light-brown curls covered her mons and around the opening of her sex-lips she had been laid bare. As she had dreaded, the tender tip of her bud was clearly visible. At this moment it was swollen and looked as hard and shiny as a bead. How indecent, wanton and delicious it looked.

'I'll have to get used to seeing myself like this . . .' she began, resisting the urge to put down a hand to cover herself.

'I think is beautiful,' Giovanni said firmly, whisking away the traces of his work and wiping her thighs with a damp tissue.

In a moment he began rubbing a tiny amount of oil into the remaining hair on her mons. Dipping beneath her body, he reached into the crease of her buttocks and anointed the tender skin there too.

'I leave you this oil. It soften and perfume all your pussy. Make all of her very beautiful and sweet. Your lovers like, I think.'

Marika smiled. She liked the way he spoke about her sex. Pussy was a word that at the same time was both friendly and intimate. The oil smelt musky. It was pleasant on her skin and did not sting her sensitive membranes.

'Now you relax,' Giovanni said, wiping his hands on a clean towel. 'Please to lie down.'

She felt anything but relaxed, but she lay face down on the cloth. The erotic tension within her throbbed and pulsed. She tried to concentrate on the feeling of the fabric against her skin. It was cool and smooth in contrast to Giovanni's warm hands which were even now beginning to stroke firmly up the backs of her legs.

She bit her lip as he massaged her. Every touch, every lifting and rolling of supple skin over toned muscle, added to the desire simmering within her. She squeezed her buttocks together, pressing her aching mons onto the surface of the cloth beneath her.

Surely he knew that she was highly aroused. Again she wondered about the limits of the service he offered. His hands were driving her crazy. She moaned softly as his thumbs pressed into the dimples at the base of her spine. Now and then the heels of his hands grazed the insides of her thighs as they squeezed and moulded her flesh.

She felt a sort of panic at the thought that her two hour limit must be approaching. Surely he wasn't going to leave her in this state? Propping herself up on her elbows she looked over one shoulder at him.

'Giovanni?' she said, calling him by name for the first time and liking the musical sound of it. 'Do you expect to give your customers *total* bodily pleasure?'

She let him see the need and desire in her eyes.

'Giovanni?' she said again, this time in a husky whisper.

He gave a sort of strangled gasp and pressed his hot mouth to her buttocks. She assumed that the gesture was the Italian equivalent of 'I thought you'd never ask!' She could hardly contain an answering groan of need and twisted around so that she was lying beneath him.

Sliding down her body Giovanni kissed her stomach, then placed a hand on each hip. Delicately he began licking the swollen tip of her wantonly exposed clitoris.

'Oh my God . . .' Marika breathed, pressing the back of her hand to her mouth. The sensation was exquisite.

She was hardly aware that the door had opened and Pia had walked into the bedroom. The first she knew of her presence was the shadow that fell across the bed and the voice, throaty and tinged with amusement, saying 'How delightful. Seems that I'm just in time for the finale.'

Marika surfaced long enough to acknowledge Pia's presence.

'Hello my darling,' she whispered. 'This is *so* much better than a box of chocolates.'

Giovanni had not paused in his movements and she arched her back, pressing her swollen folds against his hot mouth as he sucked gently at her sensitive bud. Pia threw herself onto the bed and lay beside Marika, stroking her hair and whispering encouragements as Giovanni coaxed Marika towards her climax.

I ought to feel ashamed by my lack of control, Marika thought. And by the fact that Giovanni was completely unfazed by the interruption. But instead she felt deeply excited. Part of the excitement was provided by Pia. Knowing that the other woman was enjoying watching added an extra dimension to Marika's arousal.

Giovanni was totally absorbed in the act of giving her pleasure. He held her sex-lips closed, almost pinching them together, while he lashed her protruding tip with his tongue. All sensation seemed to have centred in that tiny, aching morsel. Each stroke sent threads of pleasure to coil in her belly. Marika tossed her head from side to side, surging up off the bed and grinding her hips. She was almost there. Her thighs and buttocks tensed as she strained for realease.

Then Pia gave a sort of strangled sigh and bent down to claim Marika's mouth.

It was too much. The joint sensations of mouths on her most sensitive membranes tipped Marika over the edge. She clutched at Pia, breathing in her perfume, tasting her mouth, thrashing her tongue against the other woman's as the spasms of an intense orgasm spread outwards from her womb. It seemed to go on and on and she had to push Giovanni away finally, as even his slightest touch was painful on her super-sensitive clitoris.

Giovanni stood up, his enormous erection tenting the towel.

'I give satisfaction?' he asked, unnecessarily.

'Oh, yes,' Marika breathed. 'Complete satisfaction.'

She felt absolutely exhausted. After two hours of the most concentrated bliss, it was all she could do to roll over onto her side and snuggle up against the piled cushions. Pia dropped a light kiss on her hair, while reaching out to lay a hand on Giovanni's muscled arm.

'Oh dear, look what Marika's done to you,' she said.

Giovanni grinned. One of his hands strayed to his groin and began stroking his tumescence. The shape of his cock was plainly visible through the towel as he pulled the fabric taut. Pia's mouth drew into a pout as she looked at the fat glans and the pronounced ridge around the cock-head. Giovanni cast a regretful look at Marika and then looked hopefully at Pia.

She laughed huskily.

'Poor Giovanni's near to bursting. Someone ought to take pity on him. And if you don't want to take full advantage of his special talents, Marika, then I might have to.'

'Be my guest,' Marika murmured. 'But won't Giovanni mind?'

Giovanni grinned as he climbed onto the bed. 'It is my pleasure to *give* pleasure to both signorinas.'

Pia slipped off her tights and panties and rolled her dress up above her waist. She opened a drawer in the bedside cabinet, took out a condom, then watched Giovanni roll the rubber down his thick shaft.

'Watching you two has made me as horny as hell,' she said, reaching out to muss Marika's hair. 'And it seems a shame to waste an opportunity.'

Marika propped herself up on a cushion, watching as Giovanni positioned himself between Pia's long, slim legs. Pia's hands clutched at his muscular buttocks, drawing his cock into her eager body without preamble and grinding herself against him. In a moment Giovanni began thrusting strongly, his covered cock angling downwards into Pia's upturned pelvis.

The desire stirred and began to re-awaken in Marika's body. She had thought that she was satiated, but watching the two beautifully formed bodies straining together in the primeval act of love made her feel hot and excited all over again. They were kissing passionately now, their hands all over each other. Each of them was wrapped inside their own private world of sensation.

Giovanni slowed his strokes, holding back until Pia's breath came in short gasps and her hands slid across his broad back. When she uttered a series of sharp little cries, he drew partway out of her and used his big glans to thrust rapidly into her entrance. Pia went wild, her legs scissoring madly and her heels drumming on Giovanni's buttocks. A moment later she gave a long sigh and fell back against the cushions.

Giovanni finally allowed himself to climax. The muscles in his shoulders bunched as he thrust deeply into Pia. After only a few seconds, he groaned and his face screwed into an expression of pleasure and pride.

That's what you call *real* job satisfaction, Marika thought with amusement.

Giovanni dipped his head to kiss Marika on the lips, then he helped Pia to her feet and both of them disappeared into the bathroom. Pia came back into the bedroom first. Her hair was damp from her shower and she wore only a black silk slip which accentuated the darkness of her hair and the olive colour of her bare limbs.

Climbing onto the bed she snuggled up next to Marika.

'I don't know about you, but I'm too bushed to do anything but sleep. Shall we have a nap and go out to eat later?'

Marika nodded. 'Suits me. Giovanni's attentions are pretty intense.'

They kissed tenderly, then arms entwined, pulled the silken counterpane to cover them and lay down together in the nest of pillows.

A few minutes later Giovanni emerged from the

bathroom, washed and dressed, looking as immaculate as when he first knocked on the door. Case in hand he made his way across the room, smiling when he saw them in bed together.

'*Arriverderci, bella signorinas,*' he called out. 'Sleep well.'

'Goodbye. And thank you,' Marika called out sleepily as the door closed behind Giovanni. She had a sudden thought. 'Have you paid him, Pia?'

Pia laid her cheek against the hollow of Marika's shoulder. She chuckled, then murmured, 'You didn't guess then?'

'Guess what?'

'That Giovanni is a member of the society. He was sent a black card with my telephone number on it.'

Marika smiled. 'So when he contacted you, you set all this up for me – but also for Giovanni?'

'Oh yes. He's quite a new member. I think he'll go far. Don't you?'

'I do,' Marika said as her eyelids drooped and she slipped away into the borders of sleep. 'I most certainly do.'

It was dark in the room when Marika awoke. For a moment she could not remember where she was, then she became aware of Pia lying next to her.

She felt a surge of happiness. They had the whole weekend together. Just the two of them.

Carefully, so as not to disturb her, Marika went to use the bathroom. She glanced out of the window as she came back into the bedroom. The lights of Rome glittered far below. She could see tree tops amongst the stately marble buildings and in the near distance the Tiber looked like a winding, metallic snake.

She was hungry, but did not feel like going out to a restaurant. Besides, she would have to wake Pia and the model looked so peaceful in her sleep. She studied her in detail for the first time since meeting her again. Pia's natural good looks glowed. After the recent shoot, she must have asked the make-up artist to remove all traces of powder and paint and brush out whatever hair-style she had affected.

She looked very young with her undressed skin and tousled hair. One of the things that fascinated Marika and caused her the odd pang of envy was Pia's amazing sensual beauty which was tempered with a fresh, dreamy innocence. The two things together were quite devastating.

Pia had allowed her hair to grow into a shoulder-length bob. A short straight fringe accentuated her delicate features and drew attention to her dark eyes. Marika smiled as she looked at the full, Bardotesque mouth, so tender in sleep. The flutter of desire she felt still surprised her. How strange and wonderful it was to have a female lover.

She wanted nothing more than to stay in their suite tonight and she knew that Pia would prefer that too. They had so much to catch up on after all the months apart. Her mind made up, she went in search of the hotel menu and then dialled room service.

When Pia awoke an hour later, Marika had already washed and changed. She wore a white lace teddy under her silk dressing gown. Her blonde hair fell in soft waves across her shoulders.

'You've been busy,' Pia smiled, sitting up as Marika handed her a glass of sparkling white wine. She sipped. 'Mmm. This is wonderful. And there's food too, I see.'

The trolley next to the bed was piled high with prawn and avocado salad, freshly baked ciabatta, figs poached in Amaretto liqueur, and a bottle of chilled white wine.

While they ate they chatted about their respective

activities over the past months. Pia had been working hard modelling for catalogues, walking the catwalk for designer collections in Paris and Milan and going on photographic assignments. Marika talked about her PR work for various clients and then moved on to her recent work as an agent for the Major.

Reaching out, Pia took hold of the chain which Marika wore around her neck. The pearl pendant glimmered against the olive skin of her palm. She brushed her thumb across the engraved motif of entwined diamonds on the jet which was set in the centre of the pearls.

'I knew from the moment we met that you would rise up through the ranks of the society. What's next I wonder?'

Marika smiled. She knew that Pia had once been a little envious of her higher status. She saw from Pia's pearl pendant that the model remained as one of the rank and file. The motif carved into jet was that of a single heart.

'It's not all just fun and games. It's hard work studying all the information the Major has on file. Sometimes there are risks involved too.' She began telling Pia about her weekend at the Ronsard Château.

'Charles Germain sounds intriguing,' Pia said, when Marika had finished speaking. 'He doesn't sound like the sort of man you can fob off though. Are you sure that he won't hold you to your agreement?'

Marika shrugged. 'I haven't heard from him yet. At least, not directly. He sent me some flowers with a note. I suppose he'll phone, maybe write. There's not a lot he can do, is there, if I don't return his calls?'

Pia looked doubtful, but she passed no further comment. Scooping up the last of the salad dressing with a piece of crusty ciabatta, she popped the bread into her mouth. They finished the first bottle of wine with the figs. Marika swallowed the last of the plump fruit, savouring the taste of almonds and alcohol, then she got up to fetch a second bottle of wine from the fridge.

Pia lit some candles and the golden glow cast soft violet shadows over the draped bed. The wine had made Marika feel very relaxed and there was a warm, swimming feeling in her head. She lay back amongst the silken cushions, feeling as decadent as a pampered sex slave in a harem.

'Isn't it wonderful to be alone together?' Pia said, giggling. Her tilted dark eyes glowed and her sensual mouth looked soft and inviting. 'Sometimes it's great not to have men around for a while. They complicate things so, don't they? What with their fragile egos and their jealousies.'

Marika agreed. She knew by Pia's expression what was about to happen and she felt excited and a little fearful at the same time. It was almost awkward between them. She found herself wondering who was going to make the first move. Then Pia moved towards her until they were lying full length, face to face.

They kissed gently. And it was so easy and natural after all. Marika looked down as Pia opened the front of the white silk dressing gown and ran her hand across the top of the lace teddy. Holding Marika's gaze, Pia slid down one of the thin straps and eased Marika's breast free.

'Oh . . .' Marika murmured as Pia lowered her mouth and began suckling.

She cradled Pia's dark head as the familiar sweet, pulling sensations spread through her body. She loved having her nipples sucked. On occasion she had reached orgasm from that one caress alone. Pia's hand went to the other breast, caressing it through the lace and pinching the nipple into a jutting peak.

Marika put her arms around Pia, stroking her soft skin and exploring the other woman's body as they rolled together on the silken counterpane. The initial self-consciousness soon faded and they rediscovered the caresses which drove them both wild.

Marika's blood sang in her ears as Pia's long, olive fingers popped open the fasteners on the crotch of the lace teddy. Her touch was featherlight at first, questing and exploring and then insistent and more demanding as Marika's senses caught fire and she twisted and writhed in the throes of a raging passion.

'Oh God, that feels good. Don't stop,' she murmured against Pia's lips as the other woman rubbed her clitoris with two fingers while penetrating her with a thumb.

Pia was soft where her male lovers were hard, sweet and musky tasting where men were saltier and spice-smelling in their arousal. The contrasts were what made enjoying a woman so beguiling.

Uttering a series of breathy cries, she felt her inner flesh convulse around Pia's buried fingers as she climaxed. She dug her fingers into the narrow female back and kissed Pia ravenously, claiming her mouth and tongue with a possessive need. Pia kissed her back, welcoming the onslaught of Marika's tongue, her own lips soft and compliant.

When the final pulsings of her orgasm had faded, Marika's fierceness gave way to tenderness. She stroked Pia's slim shoulders and cupped the high round breasts in her palms.

'I hope I didn't hurt you. Now I want to give you pleasure, my sweet,' she whispered. 'Lie back and relax.'

Pia sank backwards as Marika pulled off her skimpy, black silk slip. The model's eyes were half-closed and looked very dark as if drugged by passion. Marika felt a sudden need to have Pia spread out before her, vulnerable and open in her desire and passion.

She picked up one of the bolster-shaped cushions

and put it under the other woman's hips. Pia gave a little moan as she felt the lower part of her body lifted up high and raised to her lover. The top half of her body sloped away from Marika and her cap of shiny, black hair fanned out on the counterpane. Marika opened Pia's thighs and looked down onto the neat little mound, detecting Giovanni's handiwork in the clipped, heart-shaped pubic hair.

She used her thumbs to open the lips of Pia's rosy sex, peeling them back to expose the delicately frilled inner folds and the erect bud that nestled within them. Pia tensed and arched her back, the muscles in her thighs bunching under the smooth skin.

'Do you mind me doing this?' Marika asked softly, thinking that Pia might be alarmed by her directness.

Pia shook her head. Her teeth were caught in her bottom lip and her hands were balled into fists. It was obvious that she was highly aroused.

'Do anything you like,' she whimpered. 'I'm almost coming.'

Marika closed her mouth on the fragrant flesh, using her relaxed lips to tease Pia's hard little protuberance and licking the entrance of her moist vagina. Pia bucked against her mouth, gasps and incoherent little cries bursting from her. When Pia's climax had faded, Marika removed the bolster and allowed Pia to lie down completely. She pressed her mouth to Pia's enviably flat belly, working her way up the still-trembling body and taking Pia in her arms.

They lay entwined until they grew calmer, stroking each other gently and kissing now and then. In a while they began to get aroused and to experiment once again with new intimate caresses. Before things got too hot, Pia held Marika away from her for a moment as she reached into the bedside cabinet.

'I bought something for us yesterday. I don't know what you'll think of . . . this, but the moment seems right to show it to you.'

She placed the object on the bed between them.

'Pia!' Marika exclaimed, amused and slightly shocked, but more than a little intrigued. 'I've never used one of those things. It looks really kinky. I don't know what to say!'

On the bed lay a large rubber cock, complete with balls. It was attached to a pad bearing three leather straps. Pia giggled at the expression on Marika's face.

'I thought you'd like it. It's quite realistic, don't you think? What with the veins and everything. Do you want to go first?' she said, her voice deep and husky.

'No. You put it on,' Marika said, intrigued and aroused by the image which sprang to mind. 'I want to see you wearing it.'

'Okay,' Pia said, sliding one of the straps between her legs and turning around so that Marika could help her secure it to the other two at her waist.

'How do I look?' she said, kneeling on the bed and waggling her hips so that the dildo bobbed up and down.

'Extraordinary,' Marika said. 'Very strange in fact. But it's really sexy.'

The big rubber cock jutting upwards from Pia's groin looked incongruous to say the least against her slim feminine body and small high breasts. Stretching out her hand Marika stroked the cock. It felt hard, but also warm and silky, not unlike the real thing.

A delighted laugh bubbled up in her throat. Pia was thrusting into the air now, her full mouth curved in an expression of proud amusement.

'You're really getting into this game-playing thing!' Marika said. 'That cock really suits you.'

'I know it does and I'm going to fuck you with my cock until you scream for mercy,' Pia said in a mock-severe voice. 'But first I want you to get down and suck it. And if you don't do it right I'll punish you.

In fact I think I'll spank that bottom of yours until it's scarlet!'

Marika felt her insides dissolve with lust. This was a new game – unexpected and full of the most delightful possibilities. How clever of Pia.

'Whatever you say, mistress!' she giggled, edging down the bed until she was lying beneath Pia's kneeling form.

Lifting her head she took the flaring glans of the rubber cock in her mouth and began to suck. Pia moved her hips, thrusting the cock into Marika's throat and rubbing herself against the pad which was strapped to her pubis.

'It's really good, Marika,' she said breathlessly. 'I think I can bring myself off, just by rubbing my clit against this pad. Oh God . . . Oh, yes . . . You have to try this.'

They took it in turns to wear the dildo, amazed at the different sexual combinations and the exquisite sensations they were able to give to each other. Finally exhausted, they lay side by side.

Marika propped herself up on one arm and looked down at Pia.

'So much for seeing the sights of Rome.'

'Do you mind missing out?'

'I'd hardly say I'm doing that! Thanks to you, my education is being broadened.'

Pia grinned. 'I hoped you'd think that. We have the rest of tonight to play wicked games with our new toy and tomorrow too, if you have any strength left. Then I'll take you to the flea market at Porta Portese on Sunday morning. They have the most fabulous antique lace and jewellery there.'

'Sounds wonderful,' Marika said. 'But right now, I'm hungry again. It seems like hours since we ate. I'm going to ring room service. What do you fancy?'

Marika caught a flight back to London late on Sunday night.

Pia had been close to tears when they parted this time and had begged her to stay on a little longer. Gently Marika had refused, explaining that she really could not afford to leave the office for any longer.

'I know you're right. I'm just being silly,' Pia said and had cheered up enough to wave her off at the airport.

Marika had felt emotional herself, but on the plane home she found herself settling back into her usual persona. Leaving on Sunday had been the right thing to do. Pia did not really want more than there was between them and neither did she. Their relationship only worked because they saw each other infrequently.

Marika had once been told that it was a mistake to get too close to the other members of the secret society. It had been Stone – her self-appointed mentor – who told her that she made things difficult for herself.

'Why do you want to transform random sexual encounters into ongoing relationships?' he asked her once in a letter. 'The pursuit of pleasure is the thing. Isn't the thrill of the chase and the sex enough for you?'

How like Charles Germain Stone had sounded. For the first time she realised that the two men *were* very alike. Not in looks perhaps, but in their arrogance and their supreme belief that their way was the only way.

Perhaps that was why she had been strongly attracted to both men.

Her mood of relaxation evaporated as she thought of the two men. Stone who she hadn't seen for months and Charles who was uppermost in her mind at the present time. She tried to concentrate on reading a

91

paperback, but her eyes skimmed over the pages and instead, found herself dwelling on something Pia had said.

'Stone? No, I haven't seen him,' Pia had answered Marika's query as they strolled around the flea market. 'The last time we met was in Tuscany, when you were with us. There's a rumour going round that Stone's disappeared. Certainly he hasn't been active within the society for a while now.'

Marika had gone cold all over. Stone, disappeared? The thought that she might never see him again was unbearable. She was being forced to realise just what an impact Stone had made on her life. And she had once been foolish enough to believe that he felt something for her too.

She stuffed the paperback into her case, having read the same page at least four times and taken nothing of it in. Clenching her hands together in her lap, she stared moodily out of the plane window.

Chapter Seven

MARIKA ARRIVED BACK at the flat in Primrose Hill in the small hours. While she unpacked she played back the tape of her answerphone.

There was a message from a girlfriend, suggesting that they meet for lunch next week, a brief call from Gwen, and two messages from Charles. He had called on Friday night and again on Saturday.

'Sorry I've missed you,' he said, the second time. 'You're obviously much in demand. Perhaps you'd like to give me a call?' He left a telephone number.

Hearing his voice was a shock. She smiled thinly. It had not taken him long to secure her phone number. He sounded friendly, but behind the even tone she sensed that he was displeased to find her out of the flat. And the way he had asked her to phone him did not deceive her. He was giving her an order.

A picture of him came to mind. His tanned skin, glittering blue eyes, and thick iron-grey hair. She recalled how it had felt to have him inside her, his long fingers pulling her buttocks apart as he drove his hard cock deep into her wet heat. No. She didn't want to think about that. But her body responded with a treacherous flutter of its own. So what if she had enjoyed the sex with him? That was then, this was now.

Damn him. She just wanted to forget him. Charles was trouble and almost certainly dangerous. She wished that she had not made a bargain with him, but it had seemed right to do so at the time.

She ought to feel guilty about lying to him, but Charles had not been blameless. He had manipulated her into making rash promises.

'Just leave me alone,' she said aloud as she re-wound the tape on the answerphone. 'I have nothing for you, Charles. It's over between us.'

Too tired now to do more than pull off her clothes and fall into bed, she put him out of her mind.

The next day at the office she was tired and edgy. Her eyes felt gritty from lack of sleep and only by concentrating on her work could she forget about the flowers and messages from Charles. But he obviously intended to make it difficult for her to forget him. The second bunch of flowers arrived in the afternoon.

This time they were birds of paradise, fabulously expensive and exotic with their tufted, bird-like heads of orange and blue petals on top of long green stems. They were wrapped in black watered-silk paper and tied with another huge bow.

Gwen whistled silently as she passed the tiny white envelope to Marika. Marika drew her fair brows together in a scowl as she took it.

Gwen stared at her for a moment, but Marika made no move to open the envelope. Finally Gwen held up her hands, palms showing.

'Have it your own way. We're all allowed our secrets. What about these?' She indicated the flowers, then answered her own question. 'Do what I like with them?'

Marika nodded, waiting until Gwen had left to find a vase before she slid a finger inside the flap of the envelope.

94

Look forward to meeting with you. Soon, Charles had written.

He was very sure of himself. Obviously it did not occur to him that she would ignore his calls. Well he would soon learn otherwise.

Fresh flowers arrived every day and by mid-week the window-sill behind her looked like a display in a florist's shop. Gwen complained that they would need to buy more vases if the gifts continued. In the evenings Marika took to leaving the answerphone turned on in her flat and only picked up the phone when she was certain who was calling her. Charles left another message and this time she heard the edge of anger in his voice.

'I'll leave my number again. Just in case you mis-placed it the last time. Call me, Marika. Do it.'

Her hands shook slightly as she re-wound the tape this time. He'll soon get tired of my lack of response, she told herself comfortingly. A man like that, rich, power-ful and attractive must have any number of women friends. She knew that she was attractive herself, some men called her beautiful, but she was not that special – not to a man like Charles.

Then, on Thursday afternoon, he phoned her at PrimeLight.

'I have a call for you from a Charles Germain,' Gwen said. 'Shall I put it through?'

'Tell him I'm out of the office,' Marika said quickly.

'It's the flower man, isn't it?' Gwen said. 'Hadn't you better talk to him? We won't be able to move for flowers around here soon. At least put the poor man out of his misery and tell him that you're not interested.'

Marika took a breath, her pulses hammering. She would have to face up to Charles some time. Gwen was right as usual. Her brand of straight-talking and common sense was just what Marika needed to make her take action.

'All right,' she said. 'I'll speak to him. Put him through.'

'Marika?' Charles said. 'At last. I was beginning to think that you've been avoiding me. But I know that can't possibly be the case. No one treats me like that.'

'Hello, Charles. Look, there's no easy way to say this, so I'm going to be straight with you. I want you to stop sending me flowers and leaving messages on my answerphone.'

'Really?' He sounded amused. 'There's no need to play hard to get. We're not teenagers. Besides, I'd have thought that we're well past the point of playing any kind of game.'

His voice was deep and throaty and she knew that he was thinking about the sexual pleasures they had shared. Her stomach did a lurch in response to the images which crowded her mind.

She had to stop this. Now. Before she got in any deeper.

'I'm not playing games with you, Charles,' she said coolly. 'I'm serious. I don't want to meet with you or to see you, ever again. What we shared at the Château was great. But it's over. Finished. I can't put it any plainer than that.'

'I admire your honesty,' Charles said. 'Most women make excuses – silly, transparent lies. At least those who've had the courage to go against my wishes have. There haven't been many who were brave enough. And they usually regretted doing so, in the end.'

Marika felt a chill creep over her. Surely he was not threatening her?

'I'll send a car for you tonight,' he went on evenly. 'Wear something stunning. Oh, and leave off your panties.'

She could not speak for a moment. His arrogance was overwhelming. He had not listened to a word she said.

96

'Didn't you hear me, Charles?' she said, forcing herself to say the words slowly and calmly. 'It's over between us. I'm sorry if I misled you, but you asked for it. You knew what you were doing when you out-bid me for those items and put me in your debt. Don't pretend that you didn't manipulate me. I agreed to your terms then, but now I retract my promise.'

She managed to laugh dryly. 'Think of it as a woman's prerogative, if you like. In my position, you'd do the same thing.'

He chuckled. 'You're right, but that doesn't change anything. I'm not interested in your feelings about this. Mine are the only ones that matter to me. We have an agreement, which you are going to uphold. Your reluctance only makes you more exciting, more of a challenge. I'm going to enjoy teaching you what obedience means. Remember – tonight, no panties. I want to think about your nakedness while we drive. Be ready by nine.'

Marika's temper rose.

'Send your damn car if you like,' she said, her voice dripping ice. 'I won't be at home. And I don't intend to let you order me about. Not now, not ever! And don't send me any more flowers!'

Before he could answer, she slammed the phone down. She was shaking. What a fool she had been to think she could give Charles the brush-off. There was no way he was going to leave her alone. She had no choice but to fight him on his own terms.

For a moment she sat still, deep in thought, her hands clasped on her black ash desk. Then she thought of a strategy. Of course, there was something she ought to have done the minute she returned from the Ronsard Château.

Her fingers moved over the keyboard on her desk, selecting a menu on her computer screen. She accessed the selected data base and saw the index she

97

required appear. Moving the cursor down the list she highlighted 'Merchant Banks'. When the display changed, she typed in 'family-owned' and 'Germain'.

With satisfaction she watched the information begin to appear. Got you, she thought. Now the battle really begins.

Armed with a print-out of the information from the computer, Marika spent the rest of the afternoon phoning various contacts. By the time she was ready to leave the office she had a file of information on Charles, which was growing fatter by the minute.

Her telephone conversations had, if anything, only made her more alarmed. It seemed that Charles had a reputation for being ruthless, not only in his business dealings, but also in his personal life. He had been married twice, both times to heiresses, one American and one Swiss. When the marriages had ended Charles had come out very well financially.

One of Marika's contacts, a stockbroker whom she had dated for a while some time back, said of Charles, 'He manages to keep within the law. But only just. There have been one or two whiffs of scandal, but nothing concrete as yet. Germain is ambitious and arrogant. It's only a matter of time before he over-reaches himself. Watch out for him, Marika, and stay clear. The man's a shark.'

As she left the office, Marika gave Gwen a note.

'If you need to contact me in the evening for the next few days, I'll be at this number. I'm calling in to my flat to pack a few things, then I'll be staying with a girl friend in Wimbledon.'

'Right you are,' Gwen said. 'There's nothing wrong is there? You look a little pale.'

Marika smiled confidently as she swept into the corridor. 'Nothing I can't handle. See you tomorrow.'

*

The days slipped by and there was no further word from Charles. The file of information on him was locked in a cabinet in Marika's PrimeLight office, but it was beginning to look as if she would not need to use it after all.

Secretly she was glad. It was discomforting to find that Charles was so far out of her league. If it ever came to the point when she needed to challenge him she knew that she would need some heavy-weight help.

No more flowers arrived. The huge arrangements of orchids, birds of paradise, arum lilies, and scarlet roses faded. Gwen removed them. Marika felt better with her office empty of the scent of flowers. The light from the window poured into the room again, unobstructed by greenery and showy blooms. She had not realised how oppressed she had felt by the tangible evidence of Charles until it was not there any more.

Having moved back from Wimbledon to her flat the following Monday, Marika replayed the answerphone tape at intervals and was immensely relieved when Charles's voice was absent. She began to relax. Perhaps he had been bluffing after all. Their last conversation began, in her memory, to take on the tone of a man who was lashing out impotently in his hurt pride.

It seemed that he had made one final attempt to impose his will upon her, but it had not worked. There was nothing left for him now. After all, what could he do to her if she refused to meet with him?

Her life settled into the rather hectic routine which she enjoyed. There were always meetings and dinners with clients out of office hours. Now and then she visited her nearby gym and worked out for an hour or so or swam in the pool.

There had been no contact from any member of the Discipline of Pearls, besides Pia, for a while and she was glad of the fact. The experience with Charles had unnerved her. The memories of her experience in Rome were enough to fuel her erotic imaginings and there was always her selection of vibrators to give her a satisfying release.

Early one evening she drove her car across to Hampstead and spent a few hours in the Major's company. They sat around the fireplace in the library, talking about the secret society and the collection of erotica.

She noticed that he seemed a little paler than usual and distracted, as if he was worrying about something. She had been meaning to confide in him about Charles, but decided that it could wait. After they had shared a glass of Calvados, the Major left her to pursue her study of the collection. By now she was something of an expert, having memorised much of the information held on disc.

As Marika was about to leave, Beth intercepted her in the hall. She held out a bunch of keys.

'The Major wanted you to have these,' she said. 'He has to go into hospital for a minor operation and he wanted you to be able to let yourself into the house.'

Marika took the keys. 'He didn't tell me that he was ill,' she murmured. 'But I thought he looked strained.'

Beth patted Marika's arm reassuringly.

'You know how proud he is. Hates to admit to any human frailty. It really is only a minor operation, but his surgeon thought it best that he stay in hospital for a few days, given his age. Don't you worry now. I'm staying with him, I'll take good care of him.'

Marika nodded and pocketed the keys.

'Thanks for telling me, Beth. Give him my best wishes, won't you?'

Beth smiled. 'I'm sure he knows how you feel about him. Now, he says that you're to come and go as you like. The housekeeper has been told and she'll cook you a meal, should you decide to stay over at any time. Well, goodbye for now, Miss Fremen.'

Marika tried not to worry about the Major as she went back and forth to PrimeLight. The next few evenings were a hectic round of social events. She did not have time to dwell on anything much at all besides work.

On Friday night, she dressed carefully, choosing an evening dress which was striking, but classy. Her make-up was understated, the pale, rose-pink tones suiting her skin perfectly.

A taxi bore her across London to Knightsbridge and drew up in front of a handsome stone building which housed a small but prestigious private Art Gallery.

The exhibition of Carol Oldston's jewellery had been planned and executed in record time. As a mark of her thanks Carol had presented Marika with a pair of earrings in silver and amethyst.

The young designer was looking out for Marika and came forward to meet her as soon as she entered the room.

'You look wonderful,' Carol said, taking in Marika's sheath dress of gun-metal velvet. The sleek knot of her up-swept hair, worn high on her head, served to show off the earrings to advantage. They hung down almost to her bare shoulders in a waterfall shower of delicate chains and chips of purple gemstone.

'I hope I'm a walking advertisement for your work!' Marika whispered to Carol as the young designer began introducing her to the guests.

'You certainly are,' Carol hissed back, grinning. 'Why do you think I gave you those particular earrings?'

The exhibition was a great success and Carol posed for photographs and was interviewed by journalists. Her beautifully-wrought designs, with their organic shapes and original use of materials, were bound to be a success, thought Marika. Marika too was photographed, her well-bred good looks and the spectacular earrings drawing many admiring glances.

As Marika slipped on her faille evening coat and prepared to take her leave, Carol told her excitedly how she had already received more orders for commissions than she could cope with.

'I don't know how to thank you,' she said.

Marika smiled and kissed the younger woman's cheek. 'No need. It's my job. I'm really pleased for you. This is only the start. The exhibition's open to the public for two weeks after tonight. Brace yourself for recognition.'

As the taxi headed back up Park Lane towards Marble Arch, Marika relaxed against the seat. She felt exhausted. It was almost one in the morning. What a busy week it had been. She anticipated lying in bed in the morning, reading the papers and drinking freshly made coffee. Maybe she would warm some croissants and spread them with black cherry jam.

'Thanks. Keep the change,' she told the taxi driver as she paid him.

The taxi sped away as she began walking towards the front door of the flats. The sound of her high heels echoed in the quiet street.

A sudden movement in the shadows made her start. She took a step back and a scream rose in her throat as two men stepped out of the shelter of a bush, took hold of her arms, and bore her across the street.

'Get off me! What do you think you're doing?' she cried, struggling to get free.

They were far too strong for her. Her feet barely skimmed the floor as they dragged her towards a waiting Rolls Royce. She kicked out in a blind panic and heard the sleeve of her faille coat tear. Her hair was shaken loose of its pins and strands of it fell across her face, obscuring her vision.

102

Fear made her eyes water and she thought she was going to be sick.

'Stop. Please. What do you want? Take my money . . .' she stammered, then her throat dried completely as she saw who sat in the back of the Rolls.

Charles Germain held the door open. He smiled, his blue eyes glittering, as she was thrust into the car. She fell against him and barely had time to right herself before the door slammed behind her and the car purred away from the kerb.

'Let me out of here!' she cried, anger giving her her voice back. 'What the hell do you think you're doing? You can't just kidnap me like this!'

Charles grasped her wrists and held them in to his chest.

'I can do anything I like,' he said smoothly. 'I'm disappointed in you, Marika. Did you really think that you could just ignore me? It didn't have to be like this. You forced my hand. Now, why don't you just give in gracefully, hmmm?'

He bent over her to claim her mouth, but she twisted her head away.

'You bastard!' she grated.

He laughed. 'I think I prefer you like this, after all, such fire and stubbornness. But you can't win, you know. Enough now. You're becoming tiresome. It's time you learned that it is prudent to obey me.'

Before she realised what he was doing, he had captured her wrists in one strong hand and thrust the other hand beneath her skirts. She spat and fought him, closing her thighs as he slid his free hand up between her legs.

His knuckles bruised the soft skin of her inner thighs as he forced his way upwards. She bit back a sob, anticipating the rough grasp of his fingers on her sex.

But it did not happen.

Grasping the silk of her panties Charles pulled them

103

down, yanking the flimsy garment free of her buttocks, down past her knees to her ankles. Despite the way she twisted and bucked against him, he tore her panties free, snagging them on the high heels of her shoes.

'That's better,' he said. 'When I give an order I expect you to take note of it. Now you are available to me whenever I want you. Think about that. I shall imagine the soft, willing lips of your sex, hidden from me only by the folds of your velvet gown.'

The electric window slid down without a sound and Charles tossed the scrap of dove-grey silk into the night. Marika flinched when he grasped her chin, but he only kissed her cheek gently, then let her go.

'Relax, now. We have some way to go. I'm taking you to meet some friends of mine.'

Marika huddled in the corner, putting as much distance between herself and Charles as was possible. She smarted under the indignity of having her knickers pulled down. It would almost have been better if he had forced her to have sex with him. That at least would have granted her the status of being a woman and she could have felt justifiably furious with him.

Now she felt like a naughty child, who had been punished for some minor misdemeanour. How horribly chastening.

Her arms were wrapped protectively around herself and she was appalled to realise that she was actually sulking. Charles had placed her in a scenario of his own making and she was responding just as he wanted her to. She might have been a puppet the way he was pulling her strings.

Her mouth set in a thin line. Anger at him and herself seethed within her. She ought to have known that he would bide his time, strike when her guard was down. His single-mindedness was almost admirable in its way.

He looked so imposing in his white evening suit,

black tie, and the shirt with its pleated, dress front. Reaching out he slid one finger down the length of her arm. She felt its heat through the thin, black silk of her coat. Her shudder was not entirely one of distaste.

Charles grinned. His white teeth flashed in the dim interior, as he drew a circle on the back of her hand.

'So you do still remember that I hold the pursuit of pleasure above all things? Good. You're going to be an interesting conquest.'

She did not reply, but she was impressed by his perception. He was right. She was becoming more intrigued, and, against her better judgement, excited by his treatment of her. How she hated the fact that she gave in to pleasure so easily. Her experiences within the Discipline of Pearls had taught her to enjoy unusual stimulation. It was possible – desirable even – to see the erotic in the most bizarre events.

Like this one.

She was still furious with Charles for abducting her, nothing would change that. But at least she was not afraid of him any more.

Removing his hand from her arm, Charles poured himself a drink and sipped it slowly. Marika shifted position, feeling the smooth warmth of the velvet dress against her bare buttocks.

For perhaps the first time she realised just *how* ruthless and single-minded Charles could be. It was almost three weeks since that phone call in her office, when he ordered her to 'wear something stunning, but leave off your panties'. But he had not forgotten those words and had just insisted that she follow those orders, however belatedly, to the letter.

Her stomach cramped with an unwilling excitement as the Rolls sped through the sleek black night. Under the dress she wore only dove-grey, hold-up stockings and a pair of strappy evening shoes.

Oh God. She had just remembered what Giovanni

had done to her. How naked and how tantalising her sex looked now. Charles had only to lift her dress to see her pouting, half-exposed labia and the pinkish tip of her clitoris. She could not hide the sight of her most intimate folds, even if she wanted to.

The sense of being vulnerable and yet valued purely for the pleasure she could bring to a man, was strange and disconcerting. She seemed to see herself from a long way off. Was this the cool, professional businesswoman used to handling difficult clients and securing lucrative deals? Or was this some creature of warped passions, who responded to a man who was at best arrogant and at worst a common bully?

She felt at once both torn by outrage at the way Charles had kidnapped her and fascinated by the complexity of her own emotions.

Charles smiled at her over the rim of his crystal glass, then lifted the glass in a toast.

'You are very beautiful,' he said musingly. 'I know that you're going to be worth all the trouble you've put me to. You're going to be quite an asset.'

She shuddered. Whatever he had planned for her, she knew that it would be challenging and some part of her exulted in the fact that she was able to rise to it.

They drove for perhaps another hour, although it could have been more. Marika had no way of knowing how much time had passed.

It was dark and warm in the back of the Rolls, the smoked-glass screen which divided the passengers from the driver remained closed. She was aware of a feeling of growing unreality. Charles was silent, only refilling his glass now and then and drinking sparingly.

She did not try to make conversation, sensing that it would do no good to ask him where they were going.

The scent of her perfume, Charles's cologne, and the faint smell of his single malt whisky tinged the atmosphere.

'We're almost there now,' Charles said, so suddenly that she jumped.

She had fallen into a light doze, but was now instantly awake.

'You remember our original agreement? That you would make yourself available for certain assignments? Now I am going to impress upon you what *available* truly means.'

Marika watched as he slipped his hand into the inside jacket of his immaculate evening suit. When he withdrew it, he was holding a long, white-gold chain. It was beautifully made and glimmered softly in the half-light of the car.

'Come here,' Charles said.

She lifted her chin as if she might refuse, but she moved across the seat towards him. He clasped the chain around her neck. The metal was warm from his body and burned against her skin. At first she did not realise the significance of the chain, then she saw that there was a length of it hanging down over her breasts.

Charles picked up the end of it and she noticed that there was an ornate circle of metal suspended there. It was just the right size to fit over two fingers of a man's hand.

Realisation dawned on her and some dark emotion twisted in her bowels. She was actually wearing a leash. Charles intended to lead her into a gathering of his friends, showing her off to them, like a trophy or some rare animal.

'You can't really mean to—' she began, but broke off when he smiled narrowly.

'Oh, but I can. I can do anything I like with you. And, if you want to please me – and I suggest that you do – you will put aside all other emotions, except obedience. Now, take of that coat and pull down the front of your dress. I want your breasts exposed. You have such lovely prominent nipples that I want everyone to feast their eyes on them and envy me.'

Marika closed her eyes briefly. She could not do this. It was impossible. She sat rooted, the shame and humiliation making her cheeks burn.

Charles made a sound of impatience and reached for her coat, pulling it off before she could resist. Then he hooked his fingers in her low neckline and gave a sharp tug. Marika gave a low moan of distress. The dress had been very expensive. She heard the fabric rip and felt her breasts fall forwards, protruding through the gap. Taking her nipples in cruel fingers, Charles pinched and tweaked until they stood out wantonly.

Marika hunched over, trying to hide her nakedness, her eyes watering at the hot smarting of her nipples.

'I see that you still do not understand,' Charles said. 'So I'll give you another lesson. Lift up your skirt. I'm going to secure it above your waist and you're going to walk into the hotel just like this.'

'Oh, no . . .' Marika moaned, thinking of how exposed she was below the waist. It was bad enough to have her breasts on show, but her sex too? It was unbearable.

'Please. Don't make me,' she whispered.

But Charles just laughed and pushed the dress up her thighs, pulling it free from under her buttocks. Twisting the hem into a rope, he reached for his tie pin and used it like a brooch on the thin fabric.

Marika glanced down at herself, appalled by the sight of her jutting naked breasts and exposed lower body. The velvet dress looked like a crumpled rag, all bunched up around her waist. Charles stroked the soft skin of her stomach, allowing his hand to trail lightly across the sparse covering of hair on her mons, before he brought it down to caress her inner thighs.

His eyebrows lifted as she clenched her knees together in a reflex action of self-protection. He tapped her thighs reprovingly and, trembling, she let them fall open.

'Wider,' he said coolly. 'I want to refresh my memory.'

Trying to ignore the fact that the car had slid to a halt and the driver was walking around to open the back door, Marika did as Charles ordered.

'Excellent,' Charles said, using two fingers to press her outer labia apart. 'I see that you've had the good sense to display your charms to advantage. Now, just a few small attentions, I think, before we go in.'

Marika tried to remain impassive as Charles manipulated her expertly, stroking either side of her clitoris until it began to burn and swell. It was plain that she was to be spared nothing. Not only did he want to be able to parade her before his friends, he wanted her to be in a visible state of sexual arousal.

The driver opened the car door, his face impassive. Marika averted her head and made a move to put her hands in her lap to cover herself.

'Don't do that,' Charles said, laughing huskily. 'You'll spoil Hanson's view. Beautiful, isn't she?'

Hanson grinned. 'Very, sir. You have impeccable taste.'

She clenched her fists, digging them into the soft leather of the car seats, while Charles stimulated her right under the eyes of the driver. Her cheeks burned with shame and she chewed at her lower lip. But she knew she might as well accept that she was not going to be allowed to retain even a shred of modesty.

In a few moments she was going to be led through the doors of a hotel and the eyes of everyone would be upon her.

She arched her back. No matter how much she tried not to move, it was impossible. Charles's fingers were too knowing, his pinching and stroking too expert. The whole of her sex was pulsing and swelling, her inner labia puffing up and growing moist.

At last Charles seemed satisfied. He gave the prominent nub of her throbbing clitoris a final tweak.

'Perfect,' he said. 'Look down at yourself. I want you to know what everyone will be looking at as you walk across the foyer and ascend the stairs to the private function rooms.'

Marika glanced down at herself reluctantly. How wanton she looked, with the whole of her almost hairless pussy on show. It resembled a ripe fig and was shockingly red against her pale skin, so full and generously offered up to even the most casual glance.

'Out you come, my dear,' Charles said triumphantly. 'Your audience awaits you.'

Chapter Eight

CHARLES STRODE TOWARDS the forecourt of the country hotel and Marika followed him, her head down.

The long, fine chain hung loosely between them and she measured her tread so that she could keep up with Charles. It would be the final indignity to have him jerk the chain.

Inside the foyer they were met by a blaze of lights and the soft murmur of conversation. Various guests sat around on lavender coloured sofas and there came the chink of glasses from the bar.

Marika had time only to notice that everyone wore evening dress. She saw one woman wearing a daring black gown which was entirely transparent except for strategically placed sequins. She swallowed hard as Charles led her towards the lounge, the heels of her shoes digging into the soft pile of the carpet.

Heads turned towards them and one or two of the guests spoke to Charles as he passed. A handsome woman of middle years fell into step with Charles, slipping her hand through the crook of his arm and pressing her bosom against him.

'Delighted to see you again,' she said, her fine dark eyes glowing with warmth. 'I'm so glad that you could come. These evenings are never the same without our founder.'

'I would never disappoint my members, Beatrice,' Charles said, gallantly. 'And I've brought along someone special for you all tonight.'

Marika managed to keep her face impassive as Beatrice studied her.

'Very fine,' the woman said, glancing almost hungrily at Marika's jutting breasts. Her eyes swept downwards to rest on the area between Marika's legs. 'Good responses. I see that you've readied her. Is she trained?'

'Not entirely. But she shows great promise. Shall we go upstairs?'

'Mmmm. Why not?' Beatrice said, her full cheeks creasing as she smiled. She tossed back her fall of heavy, reddish hair. 'Perhaps I'll sample your new speciality later.'

Marika flushed and her lips tightened, but she said nothing. They were discussing her as if she was some sort of collectable item. Walking behind Charles and his companion, she was aware of the many appreciative glances passing over her, but no one seemed in the least shocked to see a half-naked woman on a lead.

There was a lift to the upper floors, but Charles chose to take the stairs. Marika knew that this was deliberate. She was horribly aware of her stockinged legs and bare bottom, which swayed enticingly as she navigated each stair. She put each foot down carefully to compensate for the trembling in her calves.

'Ah, here we are,' said Beatrice with a smile. She gave Charles a peck on the cheek. 'See you later. I look forward to seeing your young lady in action.'

There was soft, sensual music coming from the open door of a suite. Charles paused before going through the open doorway and turned to Marika.

'Let us be clear about one thing,' he said, his voice hard and with a new edge of authority that made her pay close attention. 'I have been very lenient with you up until now, considering your behaviour. Tonight you will do whatever I order you to and, if your conduct pleases me, I shall allow you to go home to your flat. If it does not then I shall demand that you keep me company indefinitely, until you learn what obedience is. I have the power and means to do this, as you probably realise.'

Marika knew with certainty that he was quite capable of carrying out his threat. She was at his mercy. No one knew where she was. She realised her mistake now in not confiding in Gwen or the Major.

She fought down her anger. Her only choice was to go along with whatever scheme he had planned and, if possible, try to enjoy it. After all, she had learned to relish the spice of danger. It added a piquant note to sexual enjoyment.

But there would come a reckoning. She would never forgive him for abducting her. Never. It was one thing to agree to give up her will for a time, quite another to have someone force their wishes on her. She was very clear about that distinction.

You complacent bastard, she thought. You think that you are all-powerful. I'll have my revenge on you. The file is ready and waiting in my office.

Charles's mouth lifted with amusement, as if he had read her thoughts and dismissed them as the last rising of an ineffectual resistance.

'Come along, my pet,' he murmured, giving the chain a tiny, almost playful tug and leading her through the doorway.

Groups of well-dressed people stood around in the softly-lit room, the men immaculate in black or white suits, the women in designer dresses. With a shock, she noticed that most of them had scantily-dressed

113

women or men with them, many of them on leads.

One of these, a young man with dark hair, naked except for a studded belt around his waist and sporting an impressive erection, looked across at Marika and smiled. He did not seem to mind the fact that he was chained. His 'mistress', a blonde woman, with a haughty expression, saw the exchange and reached down to tap him smartly on the tip of his swollen cock. Instead of flinching the young man looked up at his mistress with adoring eyes, Marika forgotten completely.

The other 'pets' did not look distressed either. It seemed that all of them, except her, were willing participants in the erotic gameplay. In fact, according to the Major, this was very like the sort of event organised by the elders of the Discipline of Pearls. So far she had not been invited into the inner circle, but she did know that *every* person at such a gathering would be there of their own free will.

Heads turned as Charles walked into the centre of the room and Marika was aware of many soft whispers.

'Who's she?'

'Haven't seen her before. She's lovely.'

Aware of the colour rising in her cheeks, Marika tried to distance herself from all the curious eyes, but she knew that it was an impossible task. People were moving towards them, their leashed partners following. Soon she and Charles were the centre of attention.

'You're a dark horse, Charles,' said a stunningly beautiful woman, stroking Charles's arm. 'What a lovely creature you have there.'

Marika was concentrating so hard on not reacting to any of the comments that she was unable to look closely at any of those who stood around them. Then she saw a tall figure, a man, dressed entirely in black, moving towards her through the throng. He was one of the few who did not have a partner.

She felt as if she had been slammed hard in the solar plexus. Oh God, it couldn't be. She knew that face intimately – the high cheekbones, deep-set eyes and sculpted mouth – the air of absolute self-possession.

Stone.

Somehow she kept the word from breaking from her lips. What was he doing here, walking up to her without the slightest glimmer of recognition on his face? She hung her head, appalled that he should see her like this.

'Ah, Stone,' Charles said. 'Come to have a look at my new pet? Feel free.'

Marika felt a tremor pass through her as one long finger lifted her chin, forcing her to look deeply into those sharp dark eyes. Her brows drew together. For only an instant Stone's expression changed, softening and growing tender, until she felt the emotion rising up in her throat. In a moment she was going to burst into tears, that or hysterical laughter.

Why didn't you contact me? she agonised inwardly. And why are you here with Charles and his cronies? I can't stand that you are seeing me like this.

As if he knew what she was thinking, Stone stretched out his hand and placed his fingers against her mouth, effectively stopping her from speaking. Do not give any indication that we have met before, the gesture said clearly. Trust me, his eyes pleaded. For some reason, she did.

Imperceptibly, she nodded.

Those watching grinned and she heard other whispers break out. They thought Stone was tracing the contours of her mouth. Apparently it was permitted for guests to touch the men and women who were leashed, to examine them at will as if they were human merchandise standing on an auction block.

Marika's legs almost buckled at Stone's touch as he

115

slid his fingers down her neck and began to stroke the full slopes of her breasts. Although his expression was detached again, her nipples ached in response to his remembered touch, hardening into even more prominent red-brown teats.

She tried not to flinch as he stroked her belly and pulled gently at her scant pubic floss. There was a heavy, giving sensation in her womb and she felt the moisture gathering at the entrance to her vagina. Parting her folds he slipped two fingers inside her, rotating them as if assessing the quality and readiness of her inner flesh.

In a moment he removed the fingers and dipped his hand between the crease of her buttocks, pressing gently against the closure of her anus.

Marika swayed and stopped herself leaning towards him with great difficulty. Oh God, surely he wasn't going to penetrate her ... there? She always found that action so shaming, yet so arousing. He pressed just the tip of one finger into her and the little orifice twitched in response, tightening around his intrusive digit.

A jolt of pure lust bloomed in her belly. Even in front of all these people, she could not control her responses to Stone. She was getting wetter and soon they would all see the evidence of it. The fine covering of pubic hair would not absorb her seepage. She imagined all the bored aristocratic faces lighting up as they watched the slow, silvery trickle of lubrication.

If he keeps stroking me, I'll come, she thought half-fainting with desire for him.

Then Stone removed the finger and the danger subsided. He began stroking the swell of her bottom, almost absently, as if deep in thought, while she throbbed and pulsed beside him.

It had been so long, months, since she had last seen him. He looked as arresting as ever, his dark hair, worn longer than she remembered it, framing his severe, narrow face and falling over his collar.

Let Charles give me to Stone, she pleaded silently, knowing that she would be required to service someone during the following hours. Oh, let it be Stone who uses me. There was a glazed predatory look in the eyes of all those who stood around her. She did not think that she could bear their hands on her, not now.

'What do you think, my friend?' Charles said silkily. 'Is she not sublime? Try her if you wish.'

Yes, please say yes. Marika tried to will Stone to listen to her.

'She looks newly broken,' Stone said. 'I prefer someone more . . . docile.'

He was not going to help her. Couldn't he see that she wasn't enjoying this? She felt tiny shudders trailing right down the backs of her legs. It seemed incredible that she was still standing, her face set in an expression of haughty defiance, which was rather spoiled by the fact that her lips were trembling beyond her control.

'Newly broken, yes, but she's docile enough,' Charles said, his blue eyes flickering with anger at Stone's implied criticism. 'Let me demonstrate. I'll have my pet perform for you.'

He ran his hands up the insides of Marika's thighs, easing them apart and then pressing on her shoulders until she was forced into a sort of half-squatting position. Her calves protested at the strain put on them by bending down in high-heeled shoes and the muscles in her thighs stood out starkly under the pale skin.

She felt the lips of her sex part and knew that her labia and the tip of her swollen clitoris was hanging down a little, clearly visible in the space of her open thighs. The pearly wetness must surely be evident. Any moment now she was going to start to trickle.

Charles reached down to unclip one of her earrings, then he put his hand between her legs and fastened it to

117

one of her labia. Marika could not contain a little gasp of horror as he did the same thing with her other earring.

There was a murmur of appreciation and the sound of clapping from those who stood around. Charles beamed at them and told Marika to stay as she was and rotate her hips. Her face crimson with shame, Marika did as she was told, sinking down a little so that she had more freedom to move.

It was terrible to feel the earrings pinching her aroused sex, dragging a little against the thickened flesh-lips and to have the long, silver chains brushing seductively against her inner thighs as they swung back and forth. It was far worse to feel Stone's eyes on her and to know that her body burned for him, as it had always done.

Even here, made into a foolish erotic spectacle for the amusement of these rich, powerful, and probably jaded, men and women, she could think only of Stone and what they had shared. The tears pricked her eyes as she saw the cool and dispassionate look on his face.

Fool. Fool to have lost sleep over Stone. He did not care for her at all.

She closed her eyes as she swung her hips in a wide circle, arching her back so that her rosy sex pouted at all the leering guests and the little silver chains tinkled merrily. Let them look, let them get off on watching her. The comments of the spectators meant nothing to her besides Stone's betrayal.

'Wonderful! Look at those curves. A perfect heart-shaped bottom,' someone said.

'What sensuality. She's a natural,' said another.

'Oh, bravo. Can I have her, Charles?' said a young man with fair hair who Marika had not noticed until now.

'Me too. She's divine. I lay claim to her mouth!' another man said. He was older than the fair man and distinguished-looking.

Marika straightened up slowly, her unseeing eyes looking through those gathered around her. She knew what was about to happen.

'Of course, my friends,' Charles said, as if in confirmation. 'Someone bring a table over here. Hugh and Lloyd shall be the first to sample my new pet.'

Marika swayed, overcome by a feeling of utmost shame. The blush covered her whole body, darkening her creamy skin to the shade of a dusky rose.

Both of these men were going to use her body for their pleasure. She had no choice but to let them and Jordan Stone, damn his treacherous eyes, was going to stand right there and watch the whole thing.

Well if that was the way it had to be, she would make sure that she put on a good show!

Charles tugged gently on Marika's neck chain, urging her to bend forward and press her belly to the smooth top of the table.

The wood was cool against her heated skin. At least she would not be able to see the faces of those who watched so avidly. They were drawing in close, forming a circle around her. Those men and women who wore leashes, were made to kneel on the floor and watch also.

Charles had not removed the earrings and they brushed against her inner thighs, swaying and pulling against her aching labia as Hugh, the blond-haired man, took up position behind her and spread her legs apart.

Her heels made it difficult for her to bend forward. When Hugh pressed down on the small of her back so that her buttocks were tipped up towards him, she was forced to bend her knees and splay her legs.

Marika's vision was blocked by the short, muscular figure of Lloyd who had come to stand in front of her. Lloyd began to unbuckle the belt at his waist, rubbing his palm over the tumescence which seemed barely contained by his trousers. Marika watched Lloyd's movement, acutely aware of the tall, dark man who stood to one side.

There seemed to be a space around Stone. As if he was alone, even in the room full of people. Was he watching for his own gratification? Or perhaps he thought that she and Charles were an item. Whatever his motives were they did not excuse his behaviour. He could have spared her this.

Let's see how he likes seeing me enjoy other men, she thought viciously.

'Ready for this, pretty one?' Lloyd said, unbuttoning his trousers.

His cock sprang free. It was fully erect, thick and blunt-headed, rearing up from his bush of pubic hair. Leaning forward he pressed the moist, reddish glans against her lips. Marika could smell the cock; a hint of soap and clean sweat, and the flat, singular scent of male arousal. She knew how it would taste, even before she closed her lips around it.

A murmur of enjoyment rose in her throat as she took the warm bulbous head into her mouth. She sucked strongly at it, tasting the salty fluid of pre-emission. Lloyd moaned and began to work his hips as she concentrated on the sensation of having his hard flesh filling her mouth.

Then she grunted as Hugh dug his fingers into her buttocks, pulling the globes apart and sliding straight into her. She was so wet that the cock felt wonderful. Those watching called out encouragement as Marika sucked Lloyd while raising her bottom to meet Hugh's thrusts. The cock inside her went deep, teasing out the pleasure from her sensitive membranes.

Dimly she was aware of flashes of light around her, as if little flares were being let off, but she could not concentrate on anything but her bodily responses.

She found herself enjoying the sensation of being

120

filled at both mouth and sex. Somehow, her anger and disappointment with Stone had freed her to let sensation take over. She could not think of anything but the growing sexual tension which was surging through her unchecked.

Her slack lips moved over Lloyd's cock, rimming the head and the swollen ridge around it. He was uttering guttural cries, his hands holding onto her shoulders as his orgasm boiled to the surface. Hugh began pumping his cock into her in rapid, shallow movements, the swollen glans pulling deliciously in and out of her vaginal entrance.

She loved it when a man did that, it was almost as good as feeling a cock wedged up tight against her womb. Without warning she came, deep and hard.

The inner contractions sucked at Hugh's shaft, drawing his orgasm from him in hot jets. Hugh gasped and moaned, his fingers digging into the flesh of her bottom, dragging at her flesh until her anus gaped a little under the pressure of both spurting cock and frantic fingers.

At that moment, Lloyd spurted his semen into her throat. She swallowed the creamy fluid, curling her tongue around his twitching glans, prolonging his pleasure and coaxing out the last few drops.

'God. My God . . .' Lloyd murmured as he staggered backwards, stuffing his shrinking cock back into his trousers. 'She's a treasure, Charles. A bloody treasure. Where have you been hiding her, old man?'

'Too right,' Hugh said, bending forward to plant a kiss on Marika's bottom while he removed and pocketed the used condom. 'She's fantastic. Did you train her yourself?'

Charles smiled, acknowledging the compliments, but the expression did not reach his eyes. They were chips of blue ice.

Marika felt a surge of triumph as she pushed herself

upright. He had not expected her to enjoy the experience. She was supposed to have hated every minute of it and been shamed to the core.

She glanced at Stone, who stood nearby looking none too happy. Turning her back, so that Charles could not see her expression, she flashed Stone a triumphant smile and was gratified to see that he barely suppressed a wince.

One up to me, she thought, and you two arrogant sods can go hang!

Before she could revel in her victory, Charles spoke again and the smile slid from her face.

'If anyone else wants to try my new pet, they had better speak up now. Otherwise, I've something in mind for her myself.'

The people around them shook their heads, their faces eager for whatever else Charles was planning.

Marika looked at Charles's set face and the furious twist to his mouth and felt the spark of rebellion inside her die away. It would have been better to go along with what he wanted, pretend to a meekness she did not feel. She had only succeeded in angering him.

She hung her head as Charles led her through the crowd and stopped at a raised dais, set upon a stage at the far end of the room.

'You only pretend to be obedient,' he hissed in her ear. 'Do you think I don't recognise the fact that you are mocking me? It's a bad mistake, Marika. As you're about to find out.'

He ran his hand over her bottom, as if assessing the texture of her skin.

'I suspect that you've never been properly spanked. I'm going to remedy that state of affairs right now.'

He looked across at the people who had all crowded close again.

'Who would like the honour? I intend to watch the punishment. You there. You've been taking photographs? Good. I'd like a record of the rest of this evening's proceedings. And you, Stone, will you step up here? You showed an interest in this young woman. I'd like you to be the one who spanks her. And then . . . then we'll see whether she's in need of other training.' He raised his voice. 'Someone turn the music off. We'll have silence, I think, to appreciate this spectacle.'

Marika's heart sank as the music died. Not only was it going to be Stone who was the instrument of her final degradation, she realised now the source of the flashes of light she had noticed earlier. Someone had taken photographs of Lloyd and Hugh as they used her.

And now the whole of the evening's 'entertainment' was going to be photographed. There would be a record forever of the ordeal which Charles Germain seemed bent on putting her through.

Stone sat sideways-on to the audience with Marika spread across his bent knees. All that could be seen of her was her slim, stocking-clad legs and the peachy shape of her bare bottom.

She made no sound as the first slaps landed, but her resolve to stay silent weakened as Stone's palm crashed down onto her bottom time after time. Every slap ran into the preceding one and there was hardly room for a breath between each new onslaught of sensation.

Finally Marika began to sob, digging her teeth into her lip in an effort to stop the shaming words which rose to her lips.

Stop. Oh please, she moaned inwardly, I can't stand any more. But part of her was glad that it was Stone who administered her punishment.

The expensive fabric of his trousers was warm against her belly and she could feel the muscles of his thighs flexing and loosening. His erection pressed into her belly. The bastard's enjoying this, she thought, not knowing whether to be furious or pleased. He had one hand planted in the small of her back to hold her still while he paddled her simmering flesh with his free hand. Her buttocks felt as if they were on fire and yet she was well aware that Stone was holding back from truly hurting her.

The spanking seemed to go on and on. She lost count of the number of blows, each one sounding crisp and sharp in the silence. Far worse than the pain was the humiliation of being watched by a whole room full of people.

Then it was over.

Stone helped her to stand and she turned to face the audience. Through a haze of tears she saw that many of them had become so excited by the spectacle that they were being serviced by their leashed partners.

It seemed that Charles also was unable to control his passions. Marika's lip curled with weary triumph as she saw him being fellated by Beatrice. The woman's full cheeks were bulging as she sucked and lipped him energetically, her dark eyes slitted with pleasure. Charles leaned against the wall, his hands moving gently through Beatrice's reddish hair.

Stone took Marika by the arm and shepherded her through the joined bodies. He wore a neutral expression, but she sensed that he found such wholesale debauchery faintly distasteful.

They wove past a man who was bent over the back of his male slave, thrusting between the muscular, clenched buttocks. Two women were kissing deeply while their male slaves looked on, expressions of bored acceptance on their handsome faces. Others were writhing on the carpet in a totally uninhibited mêlée of naked flesh.

Marika dashed away her tears with the back of her

hand, unmoved by the erotic posturings all around. She felt only intense relief that Charles's attention was occupied. At least with his passions slaked he was not likely to demand that she satisfy him.

Those who were still standing began turning towards the back of the room, their interest captured by some other event that was taking place there. A woman screamed with delight and there was answering laughter. For a few seconds Marika and Stone were unobserved.

He bent close, gripping her arm tight enough for it to hurt, but his hand was gentle as he stroked away the mess of smeared make-up and mascara from her cheeks.

'It's a good thing that I decided to put in an appearance tonight, or you wouldn't be able to sit down for a week!' he hissed. 'What the hell are you doing in this place and with Charles Germain?'

'I might ask you the same thing,' she said coldly, surprised to see that *he* was furious with *her*.

There was no time for more conversation. From the corner of her eye Marika saw Beatrice rise to her feet and spit delicately into a black silk handkerchief, which she tucked into the low neckline of her gown.

She gave Charles a peck on the cheek, then said, 'Must dash, darling. There's someone over there waving at me. My naughty mouth is in *such* demand!'

Charles calmly put his clothes back in order. He walked over to Stone and Marika. On reaching them he grinned, his pale eyes sparkling with malice.

'So, my friend,' he said to Stone. 'Have you given this reluctant beauty something to remember?'

Without waiting for an answer he took hold of Marika's chain and pulled her close.

'How do you feel now, my pet?' he asked, his tone light and mocking.

She had learned to distrust him in this mood. The

fear curdled in her belly. Keeping her eyelids lowered, she tried to appear chastened as she said, in a small voice, 'I feel very sore.'

'Ah, that's good. I suspected that Stone here would be too soft with you. Well, perhaps you have learned a lesson for now. Don't you ever, ever, try to get the better of me again. Understand? When I call, you obey.'

She nodded mutely, fighting with every ounce of her being the urge to rake her nails down his sun-tanned cheeks.

Lifting her chin Charles pressed his mouth to hers, thrusting his tongue against her teeth and the insides of her cheek. She felt her gorge rise as his tongue twisted around her own, tasting, demanding, claiming.

When he pulled back abruptly, she almost lost her balance and stumbled.

'Take her home, Stone,' Charles said, turning on his heel and striding across the room.

Chapter Nine

MARIKA FOLLOWED STONE down the corridor and stairs to the hotel foyer in a kind of dream. She could not believe that Charles had let her off so easily.

It was only as they emerged from the lift into the underground car park that she realised she still had her dress pinned up above her waist. Reaching down she frantically tore at the fabric, pulling Charles's diamond tie-pin free, not caring that she tore the dress further.

Stone looked amused at the way she was trying to pull the ripped velvet across her breasts. She glared at him and he shrugged and took off his evening jacket.

'Here, put this around your shoulders,' he said. 'That dress is beyond repair. Never mind, I'm sure Charles will buy you another one.'

'Really? How would you know that? It appears that you know him better than I do,' she said acidly.

The coat was warm from Stone's body and smelt of clean maleness and woody cologne. She snuggled into it, grateful that it reached past the top of her thighs and gave her back her modesty.

She still held Charles's tie-pin. Drawing back her arm, she flung it as far away as she could. The diamond glittered as the pin flew away in an arc.

'So much for Charles,' she said, brushing her palms together.

Stone gave her a searching look and seemed about to ask her something, then changed his mind.

'I'll fetch the car,' he said. 'Wait here. I'll only be a minute. Oh, you'd better have this. I hope it's yours. I picked it up before we left.'

Her handbag. She clutched it tightly, feeling a moment's panic at the thought that Charles might have kept it, along with the keys to her flat and her credit cards.

In no time at all Stone's sleek, dark-green XJS drew to a halt in front of her. He reached across and opened the car door. Settling into the leather seat, she buckled herself in, then laid her head back and sighed with weariness.

Stone looked at her expectantly, then gave a sigh of impatience when she did not respond.

'Where to? Where am I taking you?'

Of course he had never been to her flat.

'Wouldn't you rather find the first main road and call me a taxi?' she said. 'I know what a stickler you are for the society's rules. No involvement, isn't that it? Contact through phone or card and everyone keeps their secrets. But maybe all that means nothing to you now. How does it feel to have joined Charles's splinter group?'

He rolled his eyes heavenwards.

'I could ask you the same thing, but this isn't the place for this discussion. Do you want me to drive you home or not?'

'Yes . . .' she said, suddenly weary of keeping up the pretence that she felt fine and the evening had been nothing more than an unusual erotic assignment. 'I . . . I have a flat in Primrose Hill.'

Stone drove towards the motorway as the night gave way to the dawn. Neither of them spoke and the minutes ticked by. The first streaks of salmon-pink were showing on the horizon as they sped in the direction of London.

Marika did not realise that she had fallen asleep until she awoke with a jolt to find that they were cruising down familiar streets. The early morning light was thick and grainy. As Stone parked the XJS in front of her flat, she saw a milk float turn the corner of the road.

Somehow it had become Saturday morning. It seemed impossible that only hours ago she had been at the launch of Carol Oldston's jewellery exhibition. She climbed out of the car and walked the few yards to the front door. Her legs felt like jelly and she was longing for a hot bath and some coffee; hot, fresh and black.

Stone did not get out of the car. Turning the key in the lock, she looked over her shoulder.

'Aren't you going to come in?' she said with a lightness she did not feel. 'I think we should talk.'

She half-expected him to drive straight off, but he opened the car door.

As he came to stand beside her he grinned wryly and put up a hand to smooth a strand of hair back from her forehead.

'You look absolutely done-in. Come on, I'll make breakfast while you have a bath.'

It was his gentleness that was the final straw. She swayed towards him as his arms went around her. He might be slim, but he felt as solid as a rock.

The tears poured down her face as she pressed her cheek to his chest.

'Stone, oh Stone,' she wept. 'Thank God you were there.'

'You were the last person I expected to see,' he murmured. 'I think this . . . talk you mentioned is long overdue. Let's go inside.'

Marika's legs felt so wobbly that she was glad of

Stone's supporting arm as he helped her through to the lounge.

'First things first,' he said, disappearing into the bathroom.

She sat on the sofa, listening to the sound of the bath filling. Stone was moving about, opening cupboard doors, no doubt looking for bath oil to add to the running water. This was a side of him she had never seen before. He was softer, more solicitous. She liked him like this.

He emerged from the bathroom, went over to the drinks cupboard and poured her a measure of brandy. Handing it to her, he said, 'Take this with you and go and have a long, hot soak. *Then* we'll talk.'

'You will stay with me, won't you?' she said, still not sure that this was really happening.

He smiled. 'For as long as you want. Now, off you go.'

She had no strength left to argue. Meekly she did as she was told. Right now a bath sounded wonderful and all she could think of was that he was there and he wasn't going to go away for a while.

Fifteen minutes later, Marika emerged from the bathroom wrapped in a towelling robe. She felt restored to life and almost her usual self, the brandy having imparted a pleasant inner glow. The delicious smell of fresh coffee and warm croissants filled the flat.

Padding into the bedroom, she slipped on a pair of peach satin pyjamas and a matching dressing gown. It was so good to be home. The spicy smell of pot-pourri that perfumed her bedroom seemed fresh and wholesome after the cloying perfumes and the musky sexual smells of the hotel suite.

She sat at her dressing table and peered at herself in the mirror, seeing for the first time that her face was hollowed by shadows and showing signs of strain. This thing with Charles had affected her more than she realised.

While she was brushing her hair, Stone came into the bedroom. He carried a laden tray which he set down on a table next to the bed.

Glancing around he said, 'Nice room. It's cosy. Shall we eat in here?'

The bedroom with its decor in shades of grey-blue, art deco lamps and easy furniture was her favourite room.

Marika smiled. 'Why not? This looks great. I'm starving. You must have read my mind.'

She sat on the bed, leaning against the pillows while Stone poured coffee and placed croissants and cherry jam on plates. The food tasted wonderful and she realised that it was hours since she had eaten or drunk anything.

'I was fantasising about having breakfast in bed in the taxi coming home last night, before Charles came for me,' Marika said, chewing a mouthful of the buttery croissant. 'But I never dreamed that I'd be sharing it with you.'

He smiled faintly as if his mind was elsewhere. She had given him the opening to explain his long absence, but he chose to ignore it. Well, that was not good enough.

'What happened, Stone?' she said, her voice challenging. 'It's months since we last met. After you recruited me to the society, you became the main focus of my life. Whenever I went on an assignment for the society I knew that you were somehow involved with it. You know that I was obsessed with you, and I flatter myself that you were just as obsessed with me. We had something. You can't deny that. Then . . . nothing. You just faded away. What did I do wrong? Did I get too close?'

Stone had placed himself on the chaise-longue opposite the bed.

'You do have a flair for the dramatic,' he said mildly.

'And like most women you think that *you* did something wrong. Grow up, Marika. There's no mystery. I've just been involved with some tricky business deals. I would have contacted you eventually. I still have the black card you gave me. Besides we were bound to meet through the Major or one of the society's events. The old man's really fond of you, you know.'

He was lying. The explanation was too smooth, too pat by far. She felt humiliated at having opened up to him and having been slapped down so readily. So much for his softer side. This was the Stone she recognised. Cool, self-assured, and typically, avoiding all reference to everything they had shared.

But he had given himself away on one count. He must have been in touch with the Major, if he was keeping tabs on her progress.

Why then had the Major told her that he had not heard from his nephew in many months? The Major's memory might be failing. After all, he was not a young man, but she knew that he was possessed of all his faculties. It was a mystery. She would investigate that later.

She refilled her coffee cup and sipped with relish, conscious that Stone watched her thoughtfully, his straight black brows drawn into a frown.

'What's your relationship with Charles Germain?' he said after a pause.

'I have no relationship with him,' she said. 'He abducted me. I've a score to settle with that bastard.' She paused and took a deep breath. 'I'd better start at the beginning.'

Stone listened intently while she filled in the details of her weekend at the Ronsard Château. When she reached the part about the auction and the deal she had struck with Charles, he raised his eyes heavenwards.

'Then you got cold feet? Understandable, I suppose, in the circumstances. But didn't you realise who you were dealing with?'

'Of course I did,' she said defensively. 'That was the attraction at first. Charles knew all about the Discipline of Pearls. I only found out later that he'd been thrown out for gross misconduct. Usually I'm a pretty good judge of character, but I admit that I've underestimated him. That won't happen again. I'm ready for him now. I've a file on Charles at my office.'

'You're not thinking of taking him on, are you? Promise me that you won't do anything rash,' Stone said, his voice deadly serious.

She laughed nervously. 'You sound as if you're afraid of him.'

'I'd be a fool if I wasn't at least wary of him. Charles is utterly ruthless. He started his own secret society so that he is not bound by any rules but his own. You've seen what he's capable of. Stay away from him.' He clutched at her arm. 'Promise me now.'

She shook him off. 'You needn't worry. I've no wish to ever see him again, but what about your involvement with Charles? You're a member of his society, aren't you?'

Stone's expression became guarded. His smile seemed to her to be a little forced.

'Let's say that I'm thinking of joining. Even sharks have their good points, as long as you know how to handle them. But we're not talking about me. I mean it. Stay clear of Charles.'

His tone began to make her angry. He seemed to think that it was all right for him to order her about, but not to divulge any information about himself.

'Are you worried about my welfare or simply jealous?' she asked teasingly. 'Oh, of course, it wouldn't be jealousy. Not from you, the person who's only interested in sex and the thrill of the chase!'

133

He blanched and she knew that he remembered saying those very words to her.

'That might have been true once,' he said, 'but you've a way of getting under a man's skin. You're headstrong and impulsive and you have a talent for causing trouble. In fact you're the most infuriating woman I've ever met, but you're also very, very lovely.'

He stood up and began to walk towards her.

'Stop right there,' she said, as he came closer. 'I'm grateful to you for being there to help me, but . . .'

Her pulses quickened as he sat on the bed and reached for her. He hadn't been listening. His deep-set black eyes were bound by purpose.

'Very lovely,' he murmured. 'With your glowing skin and soft hair. You look like a character from a fifties film in that peach satin. Irresistible.'

She wanted to tell him to stop, to say that she knew he was diverting her from asking any more difficult questions, but his voice was hypnotic.

His lips were inches from hers now.

'Stone. Wait. I . . .'

'Shut up,' he murmured as he claimed her mouth.

She felt her will to argue with him fade away. The taste of him brought memories flooding back. No man had the right to taste that good; so fresh, musky-sweet and sexual.

He kissed her thoroughly, until little ripples of warmth spread out over her skin. Sighing she slid down to lie beside him on the bedcover, loving the way he put his arms around her and pressed the whole length of his body against her.

After a few moments he moved away and stood next to the bed. He began taking off his clothes, his eyes never once leaving her face.

Marika shrugged off the dressing gown and began unbuttoning her satin pyjama jacket. She could hardly believe that this was happening in her flat, on her own bed. She dared not think what this might mean.

In fact, she could hardly think at all. Her senses seemed to be functioning on a different level to her mind. Just watching him undress made her feel as excited as a teenager with her first lover. A hot, deep throbbing gathered pace inside her as he hooked his thumbs into the sides of his black silk boxers and stepped free of them.

She drank in the sight of him; his broad shoulders, flat, muscled belly, slim hips and oh God, his cock, rearing up proudly in front of him.

He had made love to her twice in the past, taking her from behind in a London hotel room when she had been buckled into a leather body-suit, and thrusting into her oiled anus in the back of a car while they sped along a road in Tuscany.

She had tasted his mouth, smelt his skin, could remember every minute detail about his face, had felt him surging deeply into the wet recesses of her body – but she had never seen his cock.

It was beautiful, just as she had imagined it would be, not over-long but thick and veiny, with a bulbous tip. Against his slim hips the cock looked heavy and potent. His glans was smooth and uncovered, the flaring shape of it more pronounced than if it had been covered by a foreskin.

On the tip of the cock was a single drop of clear, salty fluid. She captured it on the ball of her thumb and rubbed it around the slit in his glans. With her other hand she encircled his shaft and began to move her fingers up and down it.

After a few moments, Stone made a sound in his throat and put a hand around her wrist.

'Better stop that now.'

Marika's mouth was actually watering. She wanted to suck him, to run her tongue along the underside of his stem and hold the weight of his balls in her mouth. But she couldn't wait to feel him inside her.

This was so different to the other times with him. There was no sophisticated game-playing, no hiding behind erotic power struggles, no dallying on the borders of pleasure and pain. This was love-making, pure and simple.

She pulled off the satin trousers, trembling with eagerness for him, and lay back on the bed. Stone looked down at her, his eyes sweeping over the swell of her breasts, the slight rise of her belly, and the sweetly curving dip of her groin. His predatory features were transformed by a mixture of tenderness and lust.

Reaching out he stroked her, running his hands over her shoulders, breasts and belly, until it seemed as if every sinew in her body was softening and becoming pliant. It was as if he was absorbing her contours through his fingertips.

Her sex ached for his touch and she raised her hips, pushing her lightly shadowed mound towards him, but he only brushed against the pouting lips with one finger, then moved his hands back to her upper body. She made a little sound of disappointment and need.

'There's no hurry,' he said huskily.

'I can't wait,' she said, unable to resist the opportunity to provoke him a little. 'I've never been any good at waiting. And I've been waiting for this since Tuscany.'

His eyes clouded. 'I didn't know that it meant so much to you. But I'm here now. So stop talking so much, woman, we have some catching up to do.'

'My lips are sealed,' she said softly, holding out her arms for him. 'As long as you don't keep me waiting any longer.'

Stone sank down into her embrace, covering her whole length with his lean, tautly-muscled body. She opened her legs and tipped her pelvis up to him, opening up the deep crease of her sex and feeling her silky juices flowing down over her thickened sex lips.

Arching over her, Stone went straight into her, his cock forging a deep pathway into her eager body. Her buttocks, still sore from their spanking, throbbed and simmered as Stone pressed her to the bed. But the slight discomfort only added to Marika's pleasure. She grunted as the big glans lodged against her womb, butting it gently as Stone rocked against her.

Lifting her legs, she locked them around his back.

'Do it to me hard,' she murmured. 'Make me forget last night.'

She moaned softly as he pounded into her, filling her with his solid heat and rolling her breasts under his palms. Her nipples tingled and burned as his fingers found them and coaxed them into little aching knots.

Dragging his mouth down to hers, she kissed him urgently, putting all of her longing for him, her frustration at their separation, into the meshing of their mouths. It seemed as if both of them would dissolve into sensation.

The emotion welled up in her and threatened to engulf her. She tasted the salt of her tears on his lips and then there was nothing but his taste, his scent, the feel of him surging into her.

Lifting her hips even higher, she matched him thrust for thrust, taking each downward stroke of his rigid shaft and squeezing him tight with her inner muscles.

'God, my God,' Stone groaned, buried in her up to the hilt. 'Where did you learn to do that?'

She only laughed throatily and dug her fingers into his taut buttocks, clamping him to her body. He stopped thrusting for a moment, while she milked him, grinding her vulva against the base of his belly with a voluptuous circular movement.

Oh this is making love for real, she thought, and I know that you feel it too. Open your eyes, Stone. Look at me. I want to watch you come.

She felt him tense and his cock throbbed and jerked inside her. He was trying to hold back, but she forced him towards his climax, loving the way his face contorted as he lost control.

His thick lashes fluttered and then his eyes opened wide, seeming to look inwards as he spurted his semen into her in great tearing jets. His breath left him in a series of little explosions and he arched backwards, the tremors passing across his chest.

Christ, he was beautiful. She loved his mouth, so hard and male, but so expressive too. Giving in to the impulse to kiss him again, gently this time, she pushed out her tongue and traced the shape of his sculpted lips.

Opening his mouth wide, he drew her lips in, making little moans of enjoyment deep in his throat. The sensation of his tongue against hers, tender flesh mashing together, made her melt.

Then he was drawing his cock almost all of the way out of her and slamming in again, still hard and potent, his throbbing shaft demanding that she reach her peak of pleasure. She could not hold back and her head thrashed from side to side as she orgasmed, the pulsing heat seeming to rip through her body and flow down over her belly and thighs.

They lay entwined for a moment, the sweat drying on their skin. Their caresses and kisses were tender now.

Stone rolled to one side and pulled her around to lie next to him. Marika snuggled against his chest, feeling his heart beating against her cheek. She was drowsy now and near to falling asleep.

Dimly she felt Stone get up and go to the bathroom. He brought back a hot sponge and towel and wiped her gently between the legs. The mattress dipped as he climbed in beside her and curled around her body, his knees resting against her buttocks.

She felt warm, safe, and cosseted.

I know how you feel about me now, Stone, she thought, and nothing you say will convince me otherwise.

In a few seconds, she slept.

When she awoke, the bedroom was flooded with sunlight. She could hear the sound of lawn mowers and children playing outside; normal weekend sounds.

But nothing was normal any more. The impossible had happened. Stone slept beside her.

Marika glanced over at the bedside clock-radio. It was three in the afternoon. She stretched luxuriously, feeling a little tingle of sheer happiness. Her movement disturbed Stone. Opening his eyes, he sat up and looked down at her.

Their eyes caught and held. Marika felt her chest tighten with emotion. They did not speak but made love again, this time more tenderly and without the frantic need to almost devour each other.

They explored each other's bodies, taking it in turn to give and receive pleasure. Stone dipped his expert fingers between her thighs to explore the fragrant furrow of her sex. He stroked and pressed gently, rubbing his fingertips up either side of her swollen bud, urging her towards one shattering climax after another.

Marika indulged her passion to fellate him, drawing his hardened shaft deep into her mouth, licking and sucking him, tasting the heady, saltiness of him. She loved the tenderness of the engorged purple cock-head. It was hot and throbbing against her tongue.

Cupping his balls, she used one finger to press on the firm pad behind them, prolonging the moment when he would release his seed.

Stone moaned softly as she used her lips and fingers to coax him nearer and nearer to the brink, while cruelly denying him the moment when he would lose control. She knew how he longed to tear himself away from her mouth and plunge into the moist, warm depths of her sex.

She used all her skill to pleasure him, expressing her unspoken feelings for him through her mouth. Having Stone here, on her own bed, freed her to show him what she truly felt.

It was too much for Stone.

'Stop . . . ah, God. Stop now,' he groaned, and with trembling hands pushed her flat on the bed and knelt between her thighs.

Then he surged into her again while she writhed beneath him and the rhythm which was as old as time possessed them both.

Marika gave herself up entirely to the sensation of having his thick cock inside her. At this moment there was no reality except the pleasure. Throwing back her head, she let out her breath in a long sigh. As Stone bit down gently on her creamy neck, she convulsed at the singular pleasure of his teeth against her skin and ground her pubic bone against the base of his cock as he ploughed her silken depths.

It took longer for them both to climax, but this time they came together, collapsing in a welter of pulsing flesh. Marika's thighs were wet with their mingled juices, her fingers clutching at Stone's broad shoulders.

'Christ. That was fantastic,' Stone murmured, against her mouth, one hand cupping the back of her neck.

'It just gets better for us, doesn't it?' she said.

He nodded and moved to lie beside her, but he didn't say anything. It did not matter.

They were so close that she could see the pores of his skin and the fine lines around his eyes.

'I can't believe that you're still here,' she said, kissing Stone's cheek and feeling the roughness of his newly emerging beard against her lips.

'I said I'd stay last night,' he grinned, twining his fingers in her hair. 'You weren't in any fit state to be alone. You should know by now that I always keep my word.'

Some of her elation faded. Was that the only reason? Surely he was not here solely out of some sense of honour or decency? The events of the past few hours *had* to mean something special to him.

'My turn to make some food,' she said, springing out of bed, determined not to spoil a moment of the time they had together. 'I'll just shower. Won't be a tick.'

He sat back against the pillows, watching her with a thoughtful expression on his face.

'You really are lovely,' he said softly and with an odd trace of . . . regret?

Surely not. She suppressed a shiver. How strange that love made you fearful. She knew that he watched her progress across the room and glanced teasingly over her shoulder at him before she closed the bathroom door.

It was still odd to see him in *her* bed, his slim muscled body outlined against her sheets. She smiled with the pure delight of it.

She showered quickly, washing her hair and using some of her favourite body lotion before going back into the bedroom. Stone was not in the bed. The quilt was thrown back and she could see the indentation of his body. She could hear him moving about and smiled to herself.

Probably he was making coffee. Her mouth watered

141

at the anticipation of drinking a cup. There was nothing to rival the taste of freshly brewed coffee.

Opening a drawer she took out clean underwear, then took a pair of cream wool trousers and a teal-blue, chenille sweater from her wardrobe. She had pulled on her panties and was about to put on her bra when she looked up and saw Stone standing in the doorway.

He was fully dressed and wearing his coat. The elegant evening suit looked incongruous in the light of day.

She tried, unsuccessfully, to hide her disappointment. And knew that Stone had read her expression.

'That's a charming image to take away with me,' he said with forced lightness, his gaze travelling over the swell of her bare breasts.

There was a bitter taste in her throat. Would she always be such a fool? While she showered her mind had been full of all the possibilities built around spending the day together. But she ought to know by now that Stone's only reliable trait was his complete unpredictability, that and his passion for secrecy.

'I have to go,' he said. 'I'm sorry, but I have things to do.'

'Fine,' she said, putting on her bra and dipping her chin so that her hair swung forward to hide her face. 'I have plans too. You'll have to excuse me while I dress. You know the way out.'

'Marika . . . I . . . I would stay. But it isn't a good idea right now. There are things I can't tell you . . .'

'It's all right,' she said, managing somehow to smile. 'Don't say anything. It was good while it lasted. Maybe you'll send me a black card in the post sometime.'

He seemed about to say something else, something about the last few hours having been special to him, but she prayed that he would not. In a moment she was going to burst into tears and she wanted to be alone to cry.

142

'Remember what I said about staying away from Charles Germain,' he said. 'I meant it. For your own good, do as I say.'

'Still giving orders,' she said coldly. 'You can't resist it, can you? Everyone always has to do as you tell them to. What is it with you? You must have been a deprived child.'

His face was bleak and for a moment she regretted speaking so harshly. She lifted her chin. What the hell. He had hurt her and she wanted to hurt him back.

'I'll be in touch,' he said softly.

I won't hold my breath, she thought bitterly, wanting only to run towards him, to feel his arms around her and his lips against her cheek, but she seemed unable to move. She felt stunned by the rapid change between them. Where had the intimacy gone?

'Marika . . .' He made a move towards her, then seemed to think better of it. 'I had better go.'

Somehow she managed to whisper, 'You do that. See you sometime.'

Turning away from him, to hide the glitter of her tears, she began to dress.

Turning on his heel, Stone left the room. She heard the flat door slam behind him.

'You bastard,' she said aloud. 'Is it just that you're a control-freak? Why is it so hard for you to admit that you care for me?'

Chapter Ten

MARIKA BLEW HER nose and wiped her eyes.

She told herself that it was no use to upset herself. Stone would never change. Just when she thought they had established something approaching intimacy, he slipped through her fingers. She knew that he was not entirely cold and manipulative, but for some reason he wanted her to think that he was.

Splashing her face with cold water removed the last traces of her tears. She brushed her hair and secured it at her nape, then applied make-up. The familiar routine calmed her and she felt a little better by the time she went into the kitchen to prepare some food.

While she ate scrambled eggs and grilled tomatoes she found the events of the past few hours replaying themselves in her head. She realised that she had had a lucky escape. For reasons of his own Charles had let her leave, after threatening to keep her with him indefinitely. The fact that he had entrusted her to Stone was evidence that the two men knew each other well.

Thoughts of Stone brought mixed reactions.

The only time they seemed to be on equal footing was when sharing some kind of erotic encounter. Perhaps that was all they would ever have; expecting more was just setting herself up to be knocked down again.

After she had eaten she decided to go for a walk to clear her head. From her lounge window she could see the trees being bent by the wind and the first leaves of Autumn skipping along the pavement. It looked like rain, so she pulled on a pair of sturdy leather boots and an over-sized navy trench coat.

The fresh air brought a bloom to her cheeks and she enjoyed a walk through the nearby park. As she trod the grassy slopes, she passed couples walking hand in hand, children sped by on roller boots or skateboards. There seemed a great number of people walking their dogs.

For the first time in ages, Marika found herself envying people their ordinary lives. It was a shock to face the fact that she sometimes felt slightly superior with her upmarket profession, her smart flat, and stylish clothes and car. Her involvement with the Discipline of Pearls was a secret she relished. Normally she enjoyed the unpredictability of society assignments, the random sexual encounters adding spice to her well-planned existence.

Today her life felt rather empty.

Determined to shake off her mood of self-pity, she quickened her pace as she returned to Primrose Hill. By the time she reached home, she was out of breath and her heart was beating rapidly.

On the way back, she had reached a decision. What she needed was some cosseting, an antidote to both Charles *and* Stone. It was all very well to enjoy surprises, but sometimes she wanted to know exactly what she was getting.

There was someone she had not seen for a while who would fit the bill perfectly. Someone whose only wish was to do her bidding, to please her in every possible way.

That was all. No strings. Just great sex, warmth and a most gratifying appreciation of her company.

Smiling, she opened the drawer of the cabinet in her lounge and took out a small engraved box. Inside was a pile of black cards, plain except for her phone number embossed in gold lettering. Taking an envelope from a stack in the drawer, she began to address it, using bold strokes of a black felt-tip.

Rafael March
Harley-Mania
The Arches

She had planned to go to the Major's house that evening and there was no reason now to change her plans. On the way there she would hand-deliver the envelope to Rafael's motorbike workshop. His flat was above the shop, so he would get the card straight away and be in touch very soon.

Knowing Rafael he would reply to her summons by late Saturday night or early Sunday morning. Either way, Sunday was taken care of. She began to make plans. One sure way to distract herself from her present worries was to indulge in blatant, unthinking sexual pleasure.

And there was no one better than Rafael to join her in her chosen scenario. Now, where should she take him . . .

Using her own key, Marika let herself into the Major's house.

The air had a cool, slightly metallic feel that meant the house was empty. In the kitchen she found a note from the housekeeper, telling her that there was food in the fridge should she want any. It appeared that the woman was visiting a relative and would be back late.

146

It suited Marika to have the house to herself. There was a fire laid in the library and she put a match to the kindling, while she made herself a pot of coffee and a plate of ham salad sandwiches.

The red walls, studded leather chairs and antique furniture were cosy and welcoming. The fire crackled away merrily, giving the room a warm glow. Placing the tray on the table beside her, Marika booted up the computer and settled down to a few hours of study.

For a while she scanned the file on a man named Klietz, a director of a multi-national company in New York, who owned an extensive collection of erotic paintings. The Major had asked her to familiarise herself with Klietz's various acquisitions as there had been word that the collection would be put up for sale before long.

After an hour or so, she exited from the Klietz file and decided to take a break to rest her eyes. She strolled around the room, glancing at the book shelves and occasionally taking a volume from the ranks of books. The Major was happy for her to read any volume she wished, but she was expressly forbidden to take any book out of the house. Given the value and rarity of much of the collection, she understood the need for vigilance.

Idly she browsed along the shelves, enjoying the quiet and solitude. She took out a book of erotic verse and flipped through the pages. After a while she replaced the poetry book and wandered to the back of the room trailing her fingers along the shelves as she went.

She would not have noticed the large book sticking out some way beyond the others had not her fingers snagged against the leather spine.

Pausing, she took out the book and found that it was in fact a large box-file, its spine leather-bound to look like a heavy tome. Curious she snapped open the side fastening and began to leaf through the various booklets and documents. She realised at once that this was information which had never been added to the computer files and, as she read on, she realized why.

The box-file held extensive personal and financial details of all the members of the Discipline of Pearls. The Major must have wanted to keep this information from the casual observer, but it was hardly safe on the open shelves. Perhaps his recent illness had occupied his mind of late, for she would have expected something containing such sensitive information to have been locked away in a safe.

Bringing the box with her, she returned to her chair and began laying out the various documents on the table. Among the lists of names were many she recognised, politicians, actors, businessmen – people of high social standing along with the rich, the self-made and the international glitterati. There were a few surprises, but it was the Major's diary which really captured her attention.

At first, as she scanned the pages of neat, upright script, she felt guilty for intruding on the Major's personal recollections, but as she began to read her fascination took over.

The diary covered only the past few months and she knew that he must have many more volumes locked away. How fascinating *they* would be. She read on, the name Charles Germain jumping out at her halfway down a page. And now it was impossible for her to stop reading. She was completely absorbed for the next ten minutes.

It became obvious that the Major knew all about Charles's activities since his expulsion from the Discipline of Pearls. He suspected that Charles had set up a splinter group of his own and he had known also that Charles was going to be at the Ronsard Château. Furthermore he expressed his concern about Stone's involvement with Charles, fearing that his nephew had been seduced by Charles's daring, his devil-may-care attitude and his willingness to take the pursuit of pleasure past the lawful limits.

Laying the diary aside, she went into the kitchen to boil some water, her head swimming with all she had read.

Why didn't the Major warn me? Marika thought as she made a pot of Earl Grey tea. He must have known that she would become a target for Charles. And he had not told her about his fears for Stone either. She had thought they were close, but it seemed that the Major did not trust her enough to confide in her.

Was all this some kind of test of her loyalty?

She was more confused than ever now. Coming to the house in Hampstead was supposed to have been a restful interlude. Instead she felt as if everything was crumbling around her. She did not know what or who to believe any more.

It was around midnight when she returned to her flat. She checked every parked car in the street and each dark corner for hidden assailants, before garaging the BMW. Even so she was nervous and edgy when she entered her front door.

A message from Charles on her answerphone did nothing to ease her mood. His voice was cool and insulting as he asked her how she had enjoyed her first event.

'I have the photographs now. Would you like me to send you some? You look divine, my pet, with Hugh and Lloyd attending you both fore and aft.' He laughed nastily. 'Perhaps you have some friends or clients who would like to see you in a new and special light? Just let me know and I'll make sure they receive a photograph, with an explanatory letter too. Should do wonders for your reputation. Think about that. I'll be in touch, very soon. I have such plans for you,

Marika. I'm sure you can't wait.' There was a pause, where she could hear him breathing, then he said, without inflection, 'Don't disappoint me this time. It would be most unwise.'

The bastard. He was talking about nothing less than blackmail. If she did not do as he ordered her to, he would send out photographs to everyone she knew. He was perfectly capable of doing so.

Those photos could ruin her.

She sat on the chair beside the phone, her heart thumping painfully in her chest. There was no way out. She would have to do whatever Charles wanted.

The phone rang and she jumped with shock. At first she let it ring, feeling in no condition to speak to anyone, but when it just kept ringing she picked up the receiver.

'Yes? Who is it?' she said curtly.

'Marika? Is that you? You sound strange. Are you all right?'

'Rafael! Yes it's me. I'm fine. Just a bit tired. It's good to hear your voice.'

She could tell that he was smiling. 'Yours too. It's been a while since you sent me a card,' he said softly, an edge of excitement to his voice. 'What would you like me to do?'

Hearing Rafael and picturing his sensitive face which contrasted so strongly with his broad shoulders and strong body, she felt much better. In any encounter with Rafael she was the one in total control – the way they both liked it.

Rafael never judged her or asked her for anything. The boundaries of their relationship were clearly defined. He followed where she led. She ordered, he obeyed.

It was just what she needed right now.

She was about to tell Rafael to come to the flat when it occurred to her that Charles might be having her watched. It would be better to meet somewhere neutral.

'I'll meet you tomorrow afternoon at 2,' she said, naming a car park in a nearby hotel. 'Pick me up on one of your Harleys and you can drive me into the country.'

'Right on,' Rafael said. 'I'll look forward to seeing you. Bye now.'

Marika slept badly, her dreams all mixed up with images of Charles and Stone. She tossed and turned and awoke twice damp with sweat, her pulses racing. It was getting light when she fell into an exhausted sleep and she did not wake until past ten.

Rubbing gritty eyes and smoothing her tangled hair back from her face, she padded into the bathroom. After a shower and two cups of coffee she felt more alive.

She wrapped herself in her towelling robe and read the Sunday papers while eating toast and marmalade, keeping her mind firmly on the events portrayed in news print. The many disasters and the reports of people around the world who lacked even the basics of life were a great leveller.

But although she tried to put Charles into perspective, he hovered at the back of her thoughts like a malevolent black scorpion. Damn him to hell. She wished she had never heard of him.

She felt keyed-up and restless, expecting a phone call or a knock at the flat door at any moment, and was glad when it was time to get ready to meet Rafael.

As she sorted through her collection of underwear, she began to get into the mood for her assignment and to feel excited. The skimpy and daring garments of shiny black lycra, lace, velvet and rubber had been

151

purchased around the time she first joined the society, when she was in the throes of discovering a new sexuality.

Now she was more experienced, a mature sexual being. But the imminent meeting brought back the thrill of those heady first days, when she never knew what to expect nor what might be expected of her.

Choosing a G-string which was a mere wisp of black lace and thin PVC straps she put it on. On top of that went a black PVC basque with a lace-up front and quarter cups, which hardly covered her nipples and gave her a deep cleavage. After smoothing on a pair of lace stockings, she paraded in front of the floor-length mirror, enjoying the sense of pleasure and pride in her appearance.

The lace and shiny black fabric against her skin made her feel quite turned on. She ran her hands down her body, smoothing them over her breasts, constricted waist and the rich swell of her hips. Turning around, she adjusted the position of the narrow black strap which bisected her buttocks and pressed gently on the tender skin between them.

The thought of Rafael's face when he saw her caused her breathing to quicken and she felt the sensation of arousal intensifying. Already the crotch of the G-string was growing moist and her sex seemed to flutter and swell in anticipation of his touch. Her nipples were hard and sensitive, sending out little tingles of warmth as the shiny black cups brushed against them.

Over the underwear she pulled on a black roll-neck sweater, trousers and boots, then covered the whole outfit with a zip-up, leather jacket.

From her outer appearance no one would guess what she wore close to her skin. She liked the thought of Rafael discovering her fetish-clad body gradually, as she revealed herself to him in her own time.

As she drove to the hotel she glanced in her rear

view mirror. Was it her imagination or was she being followed? A few minutes later she was certain that she was. The same dark green 4-by-4 which had been there every time she checked had just turned a corner and was cruising along behind her. Trying to stay calm she swung the car in a sudden tight half-circle and took a route through some back streets.

The 4-by-4 passed by the turn off, then she heard a screech of brakes. The vehicle was turning around and she knew that she would not lose her pursuer so easily. She drove doggedly, concentrating on getting to the hotel ahead of the other car, but having little hope of throwing them off the track completely.

Rafael was already waiting when she drove at speed into the hotel car park. With a glance she saw that he looked a mysterious figure, helmeted and dressed from head to foot in black leather. The motorbike he sat on was huge, a glossy metal beast, lovingly cared-for and maintained.

Slowing to a halt, she threw herself out of the car and ran over to him, hardly pausing to point the central-lock remote at her car. Without a word, Rafael held out his hand and helped her to mount the bike.

'Get going. Now! Go! Go!' she hissed, already buckling on the spare helmet which had been attached to the back seat.

Thank God that Rafael was attuned to obeying her instantly, she thought, as the powerful engine kicked into life. She felt the deep metallic note reverberating through her body as Rafael turned the bike in a graceful curve and purred out of the car park and onto the open road.

They picked up speed as they crested a hill and Marika leaned in to Rafael, shielding herself from the worst of the wind which rushed past them with incredible force.

She glanced back just in time to see what looked like

a toy dark-green car turn into the hotel car park, then they were streaking away towards freedom. As she curled her arms around Rafael's waist, she curved her frozen lips into a smile.

One to me, Charles, she thought. It was a small victory and no doubt he was bound to be thrown into a fury by her resistance. But just for now, the taste of triumph was sweet indeed.

The smell of leather and motorbike oil was intoxicating; so was the speed and the sound of the beautiful machine as they sped along a dual carriageway.

Rafael half turned his head and shouted above the noise of the engine, 'What was all that about?'

'Don't worry about it,' she shouted back. 'I wanted to avoid someone. It's nothing I can't handle.'

'OK. If you're sure,' he said dubiously.

Marika wasn't sure, but she knew that she did not want to involve Rafael in her troubles. She tightened her arms around him, drawing comfort from the feeling of his slim waist and broad back.

'Where to then?' he shouted.

She gave him instructions, all thoughts of Charles and the fact that he was having her followed ebbing as she concentrated on enjoying the time spent with Rafael. She had decided on their destination the previous evening and was looking forward to reaching it.

Soon they were leaving the last of the built up areas behind them and entering open countryside. Farmland rolled away on either side, the fields tinted russet and gold by the westering sun. They left the main roads and took to narrow lanes where the trees curved inwards overhead, forming a green and yellow canopy.

The lanes were empty and Marika felt that they

could have been travelling down some secret fairy highway.

After a time she told Rafael to turn in through an open gate and take a dirt road which led to a large, brick-built barn. As they drew near they could see that one side of the barn was open to the elements. It was empty except for a few bales of hay. A thick covering of the same material covered the floor.

The Harley cruised slowly to a halt and Rafael dismounted. He helped Marika dismount too, then propped the bike on its foot rest.

Marika took off her helmet and shook out her hair, then walked a short distance away and into the shelter of the barn walls. She was conscious that Rafael watched her every movement from behind the smoke-coloured visor of the helmet he still wore.

Rafael did not speak, but waited for her orders.

'Come here,' she said, her voice low and throaty. 'And take off your helmet.'

He walked towards her slowly, unbuckling his helmet as he drew near. Taking it off, he let it drop to the ground. His pale hair, silky and clean, fell in glossy strands to his shoulders.

Marika was aware of the tension beginning to churn in her belly. It was intoxicating to be in control and to know that Rafael wished only to serve her. He was such a beautiful young man, his face saved from appearing too effeminate by a nose that was slightly over-long. He had a small gap in his front teeth too and this slight fault gave his face a singular distinction.

Rafael grinned. His lips, full and soft, looked very kissable. Her desire for him grew as she studied his slim, well-made body. She remembered the first time they had met, how she had examined his body, trailing her hands over his smooth chest and, reaching downwards, assessing and weighing his cock and balls, letting him admit to the possibility that she might

155

find him wanting.

She shivered slightly as she recalled how he had looked. So eager to please, so vulnerable. He looked a little more sure of himself now, but she would soon take care of that.

'Take off your jacket,' she said.

Underneath he wore a white T-shirt, tucked into black leather trousers. Buckled and studded biker boots reached to his knees. Rafael's bare arms were slim but corded with muscle, a legacy of the many hours spent working on his beloved Harley Davidsons.

She swept her glance over him, lingering at the crotch of his leather jeans, where the shiny fabric was tented by his erection.

'Undo your zip,' she said.

And, when he did, she walked up close and slipped her hand into the opening. Her fingers closed over the stretchy fabric of his black underwear. The bulge felt hot and heavy and she moved her fingers in a slow, insulting rhythm, watching as his eyes narrowed and the colour crept into his cheeks.

He stood with his hands at his sides as she pushed his jeans down over his lean hips, then returned to stroking his covered cock.

Rafael's fingers clenched and unclenched as she teased and massaged him, scratching gently at the ridged glans and reaching between his legs to press on the firm pad behind his scrotum. She knew that he was reliving their first meeting, feeling again the shame and the wicked delight in being used simply as an object of pleasure.

He wore a look of anticipation mixed with the slightest nuance of anxiety. Would she find him satisfactory enough to grant him the blessing of her body? Or would she just order him to perform some act of solitary gratification?

She loved to see him looking so unsure of himself. How unusual this must be for him. His good looks would normally be a passport to success with women. That was what made the game so compelling for them both.

Slowly she pulled down the stretchy black pouch of his G-string and allowed his erect cock to spring free. Rafael swayed towards her as she reached around and stroked his taut buttocks, drawing her perfectly manicured nails over the silken skin.

She could smell the flat, salty tang of his arousal and looked down at his sturdy cock. His foreskin was partly smoothed back and the tender, purplish tip with its slitted mouth was visible.

Rafael awaited her command; hers to order, hers to do as she liked with.

Such power was a strong aphrodisiac. She felt the urge to use him harshly, as she had been used by Charles. In some odd way there was a need for her to redress the balance, before she felt again strong and complete in her femininity. She took a step back.

'Go over there and lie down,' she said. 'No, don't take off anything else. I want to use your cock as it is. Lie down and link your hands behind your head.'

Rafael did as she asked. He settled himself down on the barn floor, cushioned by the layer of straw. Marika went and stood over him, one leg planted either side of his hips. A spasm of pure lust centred in her groin as she looked down onto his spread body.

Rafael's white T-shirt was pushed up past his flat stomach and his cock jutted up from the G-string which was lodged below his sac, lifting and offering up his genitals almost obscenely.

Marika bent down and pushed up the T-shirt to his armpits, exposing Rafael's muscled chest and tight, male nipples, then she began undressing.

In a moment her leather jacket lay on the floor,

followed by her boots, sweater and trousers. Wearing only her underwear she stood over Rafael, delighting in the power she had to arouse him. She rotated her hips and leaned forward so that her breasts strained against the quarter cups of the basque, then brought a hand down to cup her pubis, knowing that the crotch of her panties was dark with her juices.

Rafael groaned softly, his cock twitching and jerking as he arched his back, his eyes fastened on her fingers as she stroked and teased herself. Easing her fingers under the edges of the lace triangle, she held the fabric away from her sex giving him a glimpse of her moist and swollen labia, but withholding the full view of her vagina.

The muscles in Rafael's arms flexed as he fought against the urge to reach for her. She smiled and bent her knees, dipping her bottom towards his straining cock, knowing how much he longed to push his hard flesh into her. But he would have to wait until she was ready.

Hooking her thumbs under the thin, PVC straps which sloped upwards from her groin, she eased the G-string down over her thighs. Turning so that she was facing Rafael's feet, she bent over at the waist and slowly stepped out of the garment.

'Oh, Christ . . .' Rafael said through gritted teeth as she presented him with a view of long, lace-clad legs, perfect heart-shaped buttocks and the split-fruit of her open sex which nestled between them.

Turning back to face him, she sank down until her bottom rested on his leather clad thighs. The straw pricked her legs through the lace stockings, but she did not mind the slight discomfort. She felt wanton and daring, crouching over this beautiful, supine man like a fetish-clad harpy.

Rafael's cock reared up in front of her, flushed and pulsing with need. She reached for it, stroking the velvet shaft and moving her fingers over the engorged head, pushing back the cock-skin fully to expose the tender skin of the glans. She captured the drop of clear juice that seeped from the tiny mouth and smoothed it over her finger tips.

Bringing her fingers to her mouth, she smeared the silky juice across her lips, her tongue snaking out to taste the mild saltiness of it.

'I hope you are in control of your passions,' she said, the hint of a threat in her voice. 'I wouldn't want you to displease me.'

Rafael bit his lip, his stomach muscles ridged with the strain of holding himself back. Taking pity on him, Marika let go of his cock and leaned forward to kiss his mouth. As he tasted himself on her lips, Rafael made a sound deep in his throat. His member was crushed between their bodies, pressing hotly into the soft swell of her belly.

She reached up to his bent arms, smoothing her hands over his skin, feeling the softness of his sparse body hair. Drawing back a little she looked down at him, spread out so willingly under her. In his armpits there was a fuzz of damp, light brown curls. She rubbed her face across his chest, her mouth catching against one nipple and then bit gently into the soft skin under one arm, flicking out her tongue to taste the clean, musky spice of his sweat.

Rafael groaned again, a tortured sound, and she knew that he was desperate to come. Lifting herself up, so that she was poised above him she reached into his jeans pocket and extracted the condom she found there. Expertly she fitted the rubber over his cock and brought his covered glans towards the channel of her sex.

Slowly she moved down onto him, enclosing him completely within her warm darkness. Rafael had closed his eyes, an expression of the utmost bliss on his face as she flexed her thighs, lifting herself up and then slamming back down. It was intoxicating to ride him like this, to sheath herself on him. Leaning back and balancing herself with her hands, she thrust her pelvis back and forth.

'Oh, God. I can't . . . I'm coming . . .' Rafael gasped, lifting his head from the floor.

Even at the peak of his excitement he kept his hands linked behind the back of his neck. His mouth gaped open and his breath came in desperate bursts as he spilled himself into her.

Marika loved the moment when a man came. Even the strongest of them was weak and vulnerable then. And Rafael climaxed so sweetly. His expression brought her to the edge and she ground herself against him one final time, feeling his pubic hair graze against her soaking labia as he filled her entirely.

As good as it felt, it was not quite enough. Bringing one hand around to the folds of her outer lips, she used two fingers to rub her clitoris. Every nerve seemed to be straining towards her release as she tapped against the hot and throbbing bud. Then she was there. Her orgasm swept right through her, flowing like a warm tide across her belly and into her innermost depths.

In the aftermath of passion, she felt tender towards Rafael and it was natural to lie beside him and gather him in her arms. They pulled their leather jackets around them and then Rafael lay with his head on Marika's breast, his hand running gently up and down her stomach.

'Do you want to tell me now?' he said, after a while.

'Tell you what?' Marika said, although she knew perfectly well what he was referring to.

'OK. Have it your own way. That's cool,' Rafael said. 'I was worried that you were getting into something too deeply. You were really scared back there, but the society is all about free will, isn't it? That's the way it's always been.'

She nodded, her fingers moving over the ring he wore on his little finger. The oval of jet, surrounded by black pearls was warm from his body.

'It's something else,' she said evenly. 'Not the Discipline of Pearls. Something I have to handle in my own way.'

'I just wanted you to know that I'm here for you, if you ever need me. OK? You can always use my place as a bolt-hole.'

She looked into his upturned face and felt a rush of affection for him. It was true, she *was* really scared, out of her depth entirely to be truthful, although she had a hard time admitting that to herself. Rafael had just echoed her sentiments.

She was tempted to confide in him. But no, she didn't want to talk about Charles, that would be to give him more reality, more strength. And she didn't want to burden Rafael. He had no part in her troubles.

'Just stay the way you are,' she said softly. 'You're the only man who doesn't make demands or expect anything from me. You simply accept whatever I offer. That means a lot to me, Rafael.'

He brought her face down to him and they kissed deeply.

'Do you want to go straight back to your car or come to my flat?' he said when they drew apart. His eyes were dark with concern. 'I could cook something for us.'

'I'd like that. Very much,' she said.

The thought of going back to Primrose Hill, knowing that Charles was having her watched, was not a pleasant one.

She would have to go back sometime, but not yet. It was so good to be with Rafael. He made her feel important and strong, a woman of integrity, as she knew she was at heart. Somehow contact with Charles had eroded her self-esteem and made her feel unsure of herself.

They dressed in silence, hurrying to cover themselves as the sharpening breeze was raw on their damp skin. As they walked towards the motorbike, the sweetish scent of crushed straw rose into the air mixing with the oily tang of the hot engine. The metal clicked and thudded as it cooled.

Marika thought that she would always associate those smells and sounds with peace and freedom.

Back at his flat, Rafael cooked pasta and made a salad, while Marika leaned against one of the kitchen units drinking coffee.

They ate the meal seated at his black lacquer table. She loved Rafael's flat, the sparse furnishings and black and white decor gave it a Japanese feel. After they had eaten, he poured them both large brandies. They drank them sitting on the sofa. Marika rested her head against his shoulder, feeling the warmth of the alcohol spread through her.

Rafael talked about his main passion in life, his motorbikes, and Marika smiled at his enthusiasm. Even though she knew almost nothing about Harley Davidsons, she enjoyed listening to Rafael. He spoke about the bikes with awe and tenderness, explaining that each one had its own personality.

'Just like people?' she said.

He nodded delightedly, pleased that she appreciated how he felt. As he spoke, she felt herself relaxing. The cadence of his voice vibrating through her body, his nearness, the warm flat, and the effects of the brandy served to spin a veil of almost dreamy contentment.

After a while Rafael stopped talking. His fingers were gentle as they stroked her hair. His hand moved to caress her cheek and she shivered at the warmth of his skin and his proximity. Dipping his head he brushed his lips against her forehead, but moved no lower.

He seemed unsure of himself suddenly.

'I didn't know whether you would want to . . .' Rafael said hesitantly, leaving the sentence hanging in the air. 'This is your assignment still, after all.'

She was touched by his consideration. He was waiting for her to make the first move.

'Oh, I want to,' she smiled. 'Very much.'

Reaching for his hand she led him over to the broad futon base that served as his bed. He stood with his hands at his sides as she undressed him, then he did the same for her.

They made love on the mattress which was covered by a patchwork leather throwover. The feel of Rafael's warm naked skin against her body was comforting as well as arousing.

He was in no hurry to enter her, intent on giving her as much pleasure as possible, using his fingers, lips and tongue to bring her close to a shattering climax. Marika bore down on the fingers which were buried deep inside her, rotating her hips as he stroked her with his other hand. Pressing her swollen sex apart he searched out the little nub of her clitoris, curling his tongue around it and nibbling at her fragrant flesh with tender lips.

He seemed to sense that she needed to lose herself in passion and spent many minutes stroking and licking her, pausing when he judged that she was near. Marika teetered on the brink, straining for the release he withheld. Then she was there. She found herself sobbing unrestrainedly as orgasm after orgasm crested and broke, ran into each other, and gently faded.

Only when she was completely satisfied, did Rafael give in to the urge to gratify himself.

She opened her knees wide, welcoming the entry of

his hard flesh. As he thrust into her, his hips working frantically as he raced towards his orgasm, she trailed her fingers over his back feeling the bunched muscles under his silken skin.

Clinging to Rafael she kissed him with bruising force, while he moaned and thrashed against her. Linking her legs behind his back, she thrust against him, milking the creamy juices from his body.

Afterwards they dozed. Marika cuddled up next to Rafael, and curved her limbs around his body. His skin smelt baby fresh and his hair, which lay against her cheek, still had a faint scent of straw. The afterglow of their passion had not yet faded. She refused to think that in a few hours she must get dressed and ask Rafael to take her home.

Marika held on tight to Rafael, as the motorbike sped towards the hotel car park. It would be light soon. Before long she would be driving to her dockland office.

Please God, don't let there be any messages or flowers from Charles, she thought. She groaned aloud. Her sense of well-being was fast evaporating. The afternoon's interlude, however pleasurable, had been only too brief.

There was no way that she could avoid Charles in the future. He knew where she worked, where she lived, and now he had the means to force her to do whatever he wished.

A cold knot of fear grew inside her, but she was aware also of her rising anger.

There *had* to be something she could do. If only the Major was his normal self and not convalescing after his operation he might have helped. She dared not appeal to Stone. He was far too involved with Charles and his loyalty was therefore suspect. Besides, they had not parted on the best of terms.

164

As they neared the hotel, she told Rafael to pull over into a lay-by some distance from the car park.

The motorbike purred to a halt and she dismounted.

'I'll walk from here,' she said, smiling at the look of concern in his eyes. 'Don't worry. I'll be fine.'

Unbuckling her helmet, she passed it to him, then leaned forward to brush his mouth with her lips. It was a chaste kiss and she smiled inwardly at his look of disappointment.

'I want you to stay hungry,' she joked. 'That way you'll be eager for more of me.'

'You're the choicest dish there is, baby,' he joked, putting on a fake American accent. 'I'll always be eager.'

He flashed her a grin as he opened the throttle of the Harley.

'Until next time, then,' he shouted above the roar of the engine. 'And don't forget what I said. Any time. OK?'

She waved after him as the motorbike streaked away down the road, grateful that he had not been moved to pry into her affairs. His unconditional offer of help and friendship meant a lot, even though she knew that she would not take him up on it.

As she walked towards the car park she tried to quell the sinking feeling in her innards. Let them be gone, she prayed silently.

But the dark green 4-by-4 was parked some distance from her BMW, just as she had known it would be. Steeling herself not to alter her stride or to flinch, she strode boldly up to her car.

Opening the car door, she put one foot inside, then, just before she settled herself into the driver's seat, she looked across at the other vehicle. She could see the shadowy figures of two men through the tinted windscreen. Somehow she forced a smile, although her lips felt numb. On impulse she lifted her hand and gave a jaunty wave.

'Sorry if you've been bored,' she called out. 'But I'm back now. I'm going to my flat. I'm sure you know where that is.'

There. That ought to give them something to think about.

She felt pleased with herself and doubted whether they would tell Charles that she had discovered the fact that he was having her followed. Charles was certainly not the sort of man to appreciate failure in his employees.

She gunned the engine of her car and drove off in the direction of her flat. With a certain grim satisfaction she saw the 4-by-4 pull out and follow her. Let them. They had no idea where she had been for the past few hours.

That, at least, was her secret. But as she neared her flat she felt her apprehension returning. As quickly as possible, she garaged the car and slipped inside the front door of the main building.

Once inside her flat, she breathed a sigh of relief. No one could get to her now. From her window she could see that the 4-by-4 was parked across the street, a silent, threatening presence.

She clenched her hands into fists, the nails cutting into her palms as she fought against tears. How dare any man make her feel like this?

Somehow there just had to be a way to beat Charles. No one was omnipotent.

Chapter Eleven

MARIKA THREW HERSELF into her work with frenzied determination.

New clients sought her out regularly, vying for her special attentions, and her diary was filled with breakfast and lunch-time meetings.

'You're not looking yourself, you know,' Gwen said, peering at her closely. 'I hope you're not sickening for flu. There's a lot of it around at the moment.'

'I'm fine, Gwen, really,' Marika said, making the effort to smile brightly. 'I expect I've been having too many late nights, that's all.'

Gwen inclined her eyes heavenwards, her mouth lifting at the corners. 'What it is to be popular. I should be careful if I were you. You don't want to wear it out!'

It was a moment before Marika realised what Gwen had said, then she laughed until her sides ached. Gwen was priceless. Her acid-tinted humour was just what she needed at that moment.

Mid-week, Gwen put through a call to Marika's office from Rob Naylor, the managing director of a cosmetics firm. Marika liked Rob. They had worked together on various promotions for his company's range of natural cosmetics.

'Rob. Hello. What can I do for you?' she said.

She soon discovered that Rob was in a panic as there had been an alleged leak of information to the press about one of his company's best-selling products.

'Someone has it in for us,' he told Marika. 'The whole thing's a pack of lies. We stopped animal testing a while back in the eighties and our new products abide by the five-year rolling rule. It has to be a smear campaign from one of our competitors. But how do I fight this?'

Marika spoke to him at length, her voice soft and authoritative. Gradually Rob calmed a little, but he was still pretty agitated. Nothing she said would reassure him completely. Finally she arranged to meet him that evening to discuss the problem over dinner. She named a restaurant in the West End.

'I'll have a strategy worked out by then,' she told him. 'And I'll get straight on to our people in crisis management. Don't worry, Rob. I'm sure we can help you.'

'I certainly hope so,' he said. 'I know that I can prove this whole thing's a set-up. But mud tends to stick, doesn't it? We stand to lose a great deal of money over this.' He paused and she could tell that he was smiling when he said, 'I suppose there's one plus in all this mess.'

'Oh, what's that?'

'I get to have dinner with you.'

She laughed, enjoying the flattery. Rob was a genuinely nice guy and any such comments on his part were light-hearted and free of sleaze; more than could be said for a lot of men. He was happily married, and, although not averse to flirting with an attractive woman, he did not 'play around'. A rare animal indeed.

'See you at eight-thirty?' she said. 'I'll have Gwen book us a table and confirm it with your secretary. Bye now.'

Marika left the PrimeLight offices early, so that she had time to bathe and get ready for her meeting.

On the way home she called into a branch of the Body Shop and bought a bottle of bath oil containing a mixture of relaxing essential oils. It smelt heavenly and she could not wait to lie back in her bath and let the fragrant steam waft around her.

She battled through the usual traffic jams, her mind taken up by all that had happened to her lately, and reached home without any memory of how she got there. It seemed that she had been driving on auto-pilot, a frightening thought.

Closing the flat door behind her, she threw her car keys and handbag on to the hall table. While at the office she could put aside her worries about Charles, once outside he loomed like a spectre in her thoughts.

She had brought home the file on Charles and while the bath filled she examined it, searching for anything she could use against him, but the task seemed daunting. Charles was very influential, extremely wealthy, and with many high-powered friends. That might not have been enough to make her back off, but Stone's words kept coming back to her.

He had warned her away from trying to take on Charles single-handed and her instincts told her that this was good advice.

She needed help. Stone's help. But her pride kept her from asking for it. Besides, she did not know where to contact him. The information in the Major's box-file was sketchy concerning his nephew, a fact that struck Marika as extremely odd, given the amount of detail there had been about most of the other members.

The most she had been able to find was a London telephone number. Her fingers itched to pick up the phone, but she resisted the urge to call him. If Stone had cared anything for her, he wouldn't have walked out after the night they spent in her flat.

The memory of that hurt still. She had thought they had shared something special, but as time passed she became less sure of that. And she no longer knew whether she could trust Stone.

Oh, what a mess it all was. Sometimes she wished she had never been recruited into the secret society.

The fact that Charles was having her followed had badly shaken her. She now regretted her one act of bravado. Whatever had possessed her to wave and shout at the men in the dark green vehicle? Charles would get to hear of it somehow, she was sure. He seemed to know everything about her and her defiance would only anger him all the more.

In a fit of despairing rage, she threw the file across the room, scattering sheets of paper in all directions.

Why am I going through all these bloody papers now? she thought.

A fat lot of good it was buying relaxing bath oils. It was no use. She could not go on like this. Her dressing table mirror showed her pale face, a pinched look around her lips and weary, haunted eyes.

Straightening her shoulders, she looked back at her reflection.

'Well,' she said aloud. 'You can't crack up now. Rob will be on his way to the restaurant before long and he's relying on you to sort out his problems. Better get to it.'

She dropped her work skirt and blouse and underwear into a linen basket, slipped on a bath robe, and padded into the bathroom.

The silky feel of the hot water and the herb-scented steam soothed her jangled nerves and left her feeling calmer, if not actually relaxed.

Marika brushed her wet hair back from her forehead after drying herself and decided to devote some time to making herself feel good. There was a good hour left to kill before she needed to leave for the restaurant. Self-massage and a stiff drink, she thought. That ought to get me in the right frame of mind.

She had decided to travel by taxi, so she was generous with the amount of vodka she poured into a glass. After adding ice and lemon, she went back into the comfort of her bedroom.

Taking a long swallow of her drink, she sat on the bed and began rubbing body lotion into her limbs. Her hands were warm as they moved over skin, massaging the honey-scented fluid into every dip and curve. She took a long time over the task, concentrating at first on moisturising her damp skin, but gradually found herself becoming absorbed in the sensuality of the task.

She trailed her fingertips over the creamy skin of her thighs and then moved upwards to cup each breast in turn. The rich lotion thinned on contact with her skin and she spread it in a slick film, moulding the full mounds of her breasts with her palms. Her nipples hardened as she circled them with lubricated fingers, lengthening into jutting, red-brown teats.

Letting out a deep sigh, Marika reached for her glass and took another gulp of the vodka. Why hadn't she thought of this earlier? Massage was a good start, but masturbation was the best relief for tension.

She brought her palms down to her thighs and slid them inwards, exerting a subtle pressure on the soft skin there. Gradually she moved towards the hot, pulsing centre of her body.

It had been some time since she had indulged herself in this way. And she decided to really go to town. Not too fast, she thought, I want to make this last. Deliberately she avoided touching the swollen button of her clitoris. Instead she contented herself with easing her labia apart and pulling upwards and outwards, so that the moist folds gaped and her pleasure bud stood proud of the surrounding skin.

Looking down between her legs, she felt a little dart of lust. Opened up like that her sex looked moist and inviting.

Her breath came faster as she stroked herself, loving the smooth slickness of her sensitive membranes. Dipping a finger into her vagina she smoothed her fragrant juices up to oil the little nub, which burned and throbbed at her touch.

A wave of heat swept over her and her belly grew taut with erotic tension. The sensations were building too fast. She moved her hand away and changed position, thinking vaguely of lying back on her bed and simply stroking herself to orgasm. But that wasn't enough. She wanted something more.

The need grew within her to be penetrated by something more substantial than her own fingers. And suddenly she felt the urge to watch herself come.

As she crossed the room and opened her underwear drawer, she felt the heaviness and the wetness of her sex. The swollen labia were puffed up and aching. At each movement her clit bucked against the referred pressure.

Moving aside the neat piles of lacy garments she took out a vibrator. It was one she had purchased especially, disliking the clinical look and feel of some models. This one was shaped and felt like a real penis. It was covered in a soft rubber-like fabric and the swollen tip had a pronounced ridge.

User friendly, she thought with a smile. It even had veins.

Before she went back to the bed, she picked up a hand mirror from her dressing table.

The satin bedcover was cool against her naked

thighs and bottom and she shuddered with eagerness as she lay back against the pillows. Bunching cushions around herself, she propped up the mirror so that she could see herself from the waist down. It was a shock to see herself lying there with spread legs, her aroused vulva on view. It seemed so lewd to view herself. She looked like a sluttish, glamour centrefold from some sleazy magazine, with her sex pouting open to view and the light frosting of brownish curls, glistening with her juices. Enjoying the fantasy, she giggled and imagined what might be written about her.

Sexy blonde ready for fun and doesn't she look it! She sure loves it, boys.

With her eyes on her reflection, she closed her legs, so that her vagina was hidden from view. The pink tip of her clitoris still peeped provocatively through the thickened lips, revealed by Giovanni's intimate coiffure. Marika sighed voluptuously. The fingers that stroked upwards over the closed folds and pinched and rubbed the jutting peak of her clit did not seem like her own. It was as if some disembodied hand, obviously a woman's with such perfectly manicured nails, was taking liberties with her. Another fantasy scenario presented itself and Marika let it flow over her. She was being held down by silken ribbons, while a bevy of lush harem beauties, trained to give all kinds of forbidden pleasures, did just as they liked with her.

She imagined the nudging sensation against her mouth as a hot, large-nippled breast was offered to her. Her lips opened to receive it and she suckled madly, while fingers pressed into her vagina and stroked the firm pad of tissue behind her pubic bone. Other fingers moved across her anus, a sharpened fingernail scraping against the tender membranes.

Oh, this was delicious. Marika fantasised unashamedly. The harem women faded and she squirmed against the bedcover, thrusting her bottom

173

into the softness of the bed as she imagined Stone, standing in the doorway of the room, a sardonic grin on his mouth as he watched her pleasuring herself. He could see the silvery moisture glistening on her labia and lightly streaking her inner thighs.

The ache she felt whenever she thought of Stone transmuted into the memory of their fevered coupling. It had been so good between them. If only she could recapture the sweetness of their pairing, just for a few seconds.

Damn him. He was inside her head, even now, when all she had in mind was the enjoyment of her solitary pleasure. But it was not surprising that she thought of him. They had lain on this same bed, meeting as sensual equals, taking and giving pleasure to each other.

And now she needed no other fantasy. The remembered reality was enough to make her senses reel. As she trailed her fingers up the parting of her sex and stroked either side of her engorged clit, it was Stone's body she saw in her mind – his face, unfocused and bound by a peculiar fragility as he plunged deeply into her body.

The images filled her inner vision, adding an extra spur to her rioting senses.

She wished that she had not changed the bed linen, the sheets and pillows might have retained a trace of Stone's smell. Instead they smelt of her own perfume. She had to conjure the singular tang of clean skin, cologne and maleness that was Stone's signature.

Moaning softly, she pressed her finger against the hard button between her legs, a whole medley of feelings welling up in her. The tension was almost unbearable now. She needed to make herself come.

Reaching for the sex toy, she twisted the base of the vibrator and turned it onto 'low'.

At first she moved the object over her torso,

deliberately avoiding her sensitive breasts. Her damp, slightly sticky skin dragged as the play-penis was trailed over it.

The ticklish vibrations spread over the skin of her arms and shoulders and she laid her head back, exposing the pale length of her throat as she moved the toy downwards, inch by inch. Closing her eyes, she brought the vibrator towards her nipples and was unable to suppress a gasp at the starburst of sensation as the rubber glans buzzed and fizzed against the turgid teats.

Oh, God. That felt good. If she kept that up, she'd come without even touching her clitoris.

Her movements had dislodged the mirror and she adjusted its position as she brought the vibrator down to rest between her legs. Gently, lightly at first she brushed the rubber shaft over the closed purse of her sex. The sensations were exquisite, tingling warmth spread outwards penetrating her lower belly and spreading across her thighs.

Trembling with eagerness now, she opened her legs and brought the head of the vibrator towards her vagina. The puffed-up lips gave against the welcome intrusion and the wonderful sizzling sensations pressed inwards and upwards. She bucked and thrust against the shaft, her hips weaving back and forth, the mirror threatening to fall over at any moment.

In the reflection she saw how her flesh enclosed the vibrator. The weeping mouth of her vagina was stretched lewdly and the puckered opening of her anus was forced to gape from the pressure. The rich odour of her arousal was pungent and she drew it in, enjoying the musky femaleness of it.

Marika's head tossed from side to side and she could no longer concentrate on the mirror. Slipping her hand into her crotch, she took her pleasure button between finger and thumb and tugged it gently. Her mouth opened wide as she cried out at the strength of her release. The orgasm seemed to spread through her whole body and smaller, lesser tremors followed in its wake.

She lay back on the pillows, arms and legs splayed apart, until she had regained her breath.

A small amount of vodka was left in the glass, diluted by the melted ice. She knocked it back, savouring the last drops of the lemony-tasting alcohol.

'Mmmm. That was pretty, damn good,' she said aloud, meaning the drink as well as the pleasure.

Perhaps it would be possible to do without men at all, she mused, if the pleasure she could give herself was that good. But it was not a real option. Masturbation was one thing, sharing an erotic experience with a male partner was altogether richer and more challenging.

She stretched, tensing all of her muscles and then relaxing them. A tingle of well-being flickered over the surface of her skin. She was tempted to have another drink, but decided to keep a clear mind for the meeting with Rob.

When she had dressed and was sitting in front of her mirror preparing to apply her make-up, she was pleased to see that her eyes were sparkling and there was a healthy glow of colour in her cheeks.

Marika saw Rob as soon as she walked into the restaurant. He sat at a window table and looked immaculate in a dark suit.

A waiter showed her to the table and Rob stood up and held out his hand. His handshake was firm and the fine lines around his eyes crinkled as he smiled.

'Nice to see you again. I wish it was in happier circumstances,' he said.

Marika took her seat, conscious of his approving glances.

She had chosen a fitted silk jacket with beaded lapels in a striking shade of mulberry. It was buttoned over a knee-skimming dress in the same colour. After setting her hair in soft waves, she had drawn it back from her face and clasped it at her nape with a chunky silver ornament. Plain silver hoops hung at her ears.

When they had ordered and the meal was being prepared, Rob scanned the copy of the proposed fight-back campaign which Marika had passed to him. She saw that he was beginning to relax and felt confident that his problems were almost over. The experts in the crisis management department of PrimeLight had come up with a detailed strategy.

The food arrived and they discussed the finer points of the campaign as they ate. Marika's peppered beef with anchovy and herb sauce was delicious, as was the accompanying salad of endive and artichoke hearts. With the meal they shared a bottle of claret. After her dessert of cherry soufflé, Marika ordered a Grand Marnier with her coffee.

Although the meeting was strictly business, Marika enjoyed Rob's company. He was an intelligent man and she admired his integrity. His company had stopped animal testing before such things became a political issue and it was grossly unfair that he was being pilloried by small-minded competitors.

They took their time over the coffee and liqueurs and it was a little after ten when they came out of the restaurant. Fine rain was falling and the roads and pavements gleamed like grey metal.

Rob hailed a cab and they shared it until he got out at the end of a terrace of Georgian town houses.

'Thanks for meeting me at such short notice,' he said, shaking her hand. 'I really appreciated it. You've set my mind at rest.'

'A pleasure doing business with you, as always,' she said.

177

Marika told the driver to take her on to Primrose Hill and leaned back in her seat to watch night-time London pass by. She was relaxed and at ease. It gave her a good feeling to know that her client was satisfied.

Getting out of the taxi, she paid and tipped the driver, almost forgetting to get a receipt, then hurried towards the block of flats. Turning up her collar, she kept her head down, her high-heeled shoes making a staccato sound on the wet road.

Despite the rain and the cold wind, she felt full of the glow of good food and wine, and her normal defences had dropped. Consequently she did not see the car until it was almost upon her.

There was a screech of brakes and the black Rolls Royce slammed to a halt, its wheels coming to rest in a deep puddle. A spurt of water soaked Marika's stockinged legs and stained the hem of her dress. She jumped back from the kerb, about to remonstrate with the driver, when she recognised the car.

Oh, God. No. Charles.

For a moment fear made her weak at the knees, then she made a dash forward, hoping to reach her front door before the car's occupants could get out. But the car door was flung wide, effectively blocking her path. A large, uniformed man got out and turned towards her.

With insolent slowness, he opened the rear door, gesturing for her to get in.

Numbly Marika shook her head. She began backing away, her mind racing. The panic was thudding in her ears. Would she have time to run around the side of the car and duck into the block of flats? Or was it better to just run for it?

The chauffeur smiled coldly.

'I advise you not to keep Mr Germain waiting,' he said.

Spinning around Marika began to run. She had no

idea where she was going. Her one thought was to put distance between herself and Charles. The high heels and smooth soles of her shoes hampered her movements. Without a second thought she kicked them off, trying not to think of the coldness of the wet streets beneath her feet.

Chapter Twelve

MARIKA'S HEART WAS in her mouth as she ran. She could hear the heavy footsteps of the chauffeur behind her. He was gaining. If only she could get to the end of the street. Someone might help her.

A stone bit cruelly into the sole of one foot and she stumbled, grimacing at the sharp pain.

Suddenly strong arms closed around her waist and lifted her body into the air. She kicked out in terror and flailed at her captor with her fists.

The chauffeur laughed, an unpleasant sound that seemed to come from deep within his barrel chest.

'Put me down!' she sobbed, raking at his face and breaking a nail. 'You bastard! Let me go!'

'More than my job's worth, I'm afraid,' he said, not unkindly, imprisoning both of her wrists in one huge hand. 'Come on now. Keep still. You'll only hurt yourself. Mr Germain just wants a word with you.'

Still struggling Marika was borne back to the car. She felt the seam of her jacket rip and her lapel was crushed against a powerful torso. A shower of mulberry beads fell to the floor.

The chauffeur dumped her unceremoniously on to the pavement, next to the open back door of the Rolls Royce. Landing on her injured foot, Marika winced and bit back a cry of pain.

The chauffeur exerted pressure on her shoulders, forcing her to bend down and look into the car's interior. Charles was leaning back against the darkness of the leather seat, a glass of single malt whisky in his hand. He had not even bothered to step out of the car, she thought bitterly, supremely confident that she would not get far.

'Still fighting the unavoidable, I see?' Charles said lightly. 'A show of spirit is to be welcomed, but I had expected you to bow to the inevitable by now. I'm afraid that you are becoming tiresome, Marika.'

'How dare you hound me like this?' she said, horrified by the smallness of her voice. 'Haven't I paid enough for the crime of defying you? You've had me followed and you've harassed me until I'm almost out of my mind. Isn't that revenge enough?'

Suddenly she was choking back tears, hating herself for the show of weakness, but unable to control her reactions.

'Had you followed?' Charles said, looking puzzled. 'Why would I do that? I already know all your movements intimately. I could have sent someone to pick you up whenever I wished.'

Marika was stunned. She believed him. Then who had been in the 4 by 4?

'Enough of this,' Charles said in a bored voice. 'Get in the car.'

'Go to hell!'

Marika dashed a hand across her eyes and pulled against the restraining hand on her wrist. The chauffeur's fingers tightened. Charles sighed deeply and leaned forward. His face was devoid of all emotion.

'You just don't get it, do you? You have no choice. You never had. I wanted you from the first moment I set eyes on you. The Discipline of Pearls was never right for you. You needed the challenge of my society. Why won't you admit to that? You could have had anything you wanted. Together we could have experienced such power, such erotic delights. But you continue to refuse me. I'm tired of your whining complaints, your ineffectual attempts to avoid me. I'm going to say this for the last time. Get in the car or I'll have Lionel here throw you in and hold you down while I give you a lesson you'll never forget!'

Reaching into the shadowy recesses of the car, he produced a riding crop. He laid the notched leather tip across his palm and began tapping it against his skin. In the gloom his eyes looked pale and deadly.

Marika recoiled from him in horror. He looked as if he hated her and she knew without a doubt that he would carry out his threat. The sound of the crop hitting his hand was heavy with menace. Instinctively she knew that he wanted to break her. He had always wanted that. Charles did not want to meet her on equal terms, nor did he want her just to be a submissive partner in his complicated sex games.

He wanted her to be afraid of him.

Oh, God. She understood now. It was her terror that excited him.

She felt her will to resist him slipping away. He was too powerful, too ruthless, for her to fight alone. But his supreme confidence, the way he had manipulated her, step by step, to this final meeting, irked her still.

From somewhere she found the courage to flash at him, 'And to think that I once found you attractive. You're nothing more than a common bully!'

Out of the corner of her eye she saw Lionel smirk as if he appreciated her show of spirit. She sensed that he was reluctant to force her into the back of the car. But she knew that he would do as his employer ordered eventually.

'Enough!' Charles rapped, white to the lips. 'I'm

going to destroy you, Marika. By this time tomorrow everyone who ever knew you is going to be looking at a photograph of you engaging in explicit sexual acts with a number of men. Your career will be finished. There'll be nowhere for you to go. And you'll crawl to me on your knees, begging me to take care of you.'

The full impact of his words hit her and she began to shake. He couldn't mean it. But she knew that he did. There were no choices left. Her shoulders sagged and she moved forward.

Suddenly a dark figure emerged from the shrubs that bordered the front of the block of flats.

'Are these the photographs you're talking about, Germain?' Stone said, holding an envelope in the air. 'Oh, I don't think you'll be using them. I have all the prints and negatives here.'

Marika whipped around to face Stone. She might have fallen if Lionel's hands had not reached out to steady her.

Slowly Charles got out of the car. He ignored Marika.

'What the hell are you doing with those?' he hissed at Stone. 'I didn't take you for a thief. Give me those photographs at once, before I forget that we're friends.'

Stone said nothing, only stood his ground and pinned Charles with cold eyes. His face was impassive.

'Oh, I get it now,' Charles said softly. 'I've seen the way you look at her. You want Marika for yourself. That's it, isn't it? And you think that you can impress her by defying me.'

He laughed mirthlessly. 'Well, well. I didn't have you down as the heroic sort either. Seems that I've misjudged you. Rein-in the white charger, Stone. The woman's mine. She's coming with me. I'm taking her where neither you nor anyone else will find her. Get out of here. You're way out of your league.'

183

'And you're finished!' Stone said in a voice like ice. 'This is the last time you're going to get your way using threats and blackmail. Is that enough evidence for you, Inspector?'

A number of plain-clothes policemen appeared from out of the shadows. One of them, a middle-aged man with a shock of reddish hair, came up to stand beside Stone.

'Oh, I should think so, sir. Threats to commit blackmail as well as attempted abduction, in front of plenty of witnesses. Along with what we already have on Germain here, regarding major business fraud, I should say that'll add up to a long stretch.' He began addressing Charles. 'I should caution you, sir—'

'Save the sermon,' Charles said acidly. 'I'm saying nothing until I've spoken to my lawyer.' He glanced at Marika, his lips curved in a smile that did not reach his eyes. 'Almost had you though, didn't I? It was fun for a while, you have to agree.'

She twisted away from him, the temptation to slap his smug face almost too strong to resist. Events had happened so fast that she felt dazed. One of the policemen told Lionel to get in the car. The chauffeur bent close to whisper in Marika's ear.

'No hard feelings?'

Marika's injured foot throbbed and the wet and cold of the pavement seemed to have crept up past her ankles. She leaned against the bonnet of the car, taking the weight off her foot. No one was taking any notice of her.

The Inspector was busy with Charles and one of the other detectives was talking to Stone. In the excitement of the arrest she seemed to have been forgotten. It occurred to her that this whole thing must have been a set up. How else would Stone and the police have been so conveniently in the vicinity?

The only thing was that nobody had bothered to tell

184

her that she was the bait to catch Charles. She did not know whether to feel angry at being used or relieved that the danger was past.

Surrounded by policemen, Charles did not look at all impressive. Should she say anything to him? No. He wasn't worth it. She turned her back. It was over. He would not be bothering her any more. That fact might sink in later, but right now she felt empty and very, very tired.

'If nobody minds,' she said with heavy sarcasm, 'I'm going up to my flat. I'm freezing, my foot needs attention, and I'm in need of a strong drink. If someone would like to look along the street for a pair of mulberry suede shoes I'd be very grateful!'

With that, she pushed the men aside and limped towards the flats without a backward glance. As for Stone – she'd deal with him later.

In the bathroom, Marika stripped off her sodden stockings and washed her cut foot. The object trodden on, she realised now, had been a piece of glass.

The wound was deep but clean. After smearing it with antiseptic, she applied a dressing. Reaction had set in now and her teeth chattered as she applied cleanser and wiped her face free of smeared make-up.

Removing the silver clasp, she brushed her hair and scraped it back, then changed out of her evening clothes and put on a pair of track pants, a fleece-lined T-shirt, and thick woollen socks. Covering everything with her thick towelling robe, she went into the kitchen and made a pot of strong coffee. By the time the police arrived at her door, she was sipping a mug of coffee, well laced with brandy.

Stone was with the Inspector. He handed her the mulberry shoes.

'Are you all right? Charles didn't hurt you?'

She shook her head. 'You arrived just in time. Rather conveniently.'

He ignored her tone.

'You're going to have to answer a few questions, I'm afraid, but the Inspector has promised to be brief. You'll need to make a statement, but that can be done later, down at the station.'

He sat on the edge of the sofa, his back to the other men who were still filing into the room. Raising his hand, he stroked her cheek.

'You look very young and vulnerable with your face all clean and your hair in a pony-tail,' he said gently.

Marika did not reply. Part of her was glad that he was there. This was the Stone she yearned for, the one who cared for her as a person and friend; not just a partner in his erotic games. But another part of her was furious with him. He was also the man who had walked out on her at a vulnerable moment. And he had deliberately kept information from her.

It was well past midnight by the time she had finished answering questions. It had become obvious to her, as the Inspector spoke, that Charles had been under police surveillance for some time and that Stone had been assisting them for reasons of his own.

She felt her anger rising as she realised that at any time Stone could have confided in her, but had chosen not to. Her agitation grew, but she managed to contain it.

When the police left she sprang up from the chair to show them out, quite forgetting her sore foot. After closing the front door, she returned to the sitting room, where Stone sat on the sofa.

'Well, here we are. Alone at last,' she said coolly. 'Why didn't you tell me that you were spying on Charles, instead of letting me think that you were some sort of traitor? Did it never occur to you that I've been half out of my mind with fear and worry, while you . . . you've been playing bloody cops and robbers! Just how long has this investigation into Charles's business dealings been going on?'

'For quite some months,' Stone said evenly. 'I wanted to tell you about it, but I couldn't risk jeopardising everything I'd worked for. I spent a lot of time getting close to Charles, earning his trust and friendship. Besides I wasn't sure what your motives were. I was shocked when I saw you with him, at the hotel. For all I knew, you had gone over to his society. Don't you see? I couldn't risk blowing my cover. It was too important to nail Charles. He had made various threats to other members of our society. I left you in ignorance for your own protection. If Charles had had the slightest inkling that you and I were involved . . . Well, there was no telling what he'd do.'

'That doesn't wash and you know it,' Marika said angrily. 'What about the night we spent in my bedroom, after Charles told you to bring me home? My God, you saw what a state I was in. I'm not that good an actress. And you must have known why Charles took the photographs. You knew what kind of man he was, even better than I did, but you let me go on thinking that I was alone and in danger. Face it, you didn't trust me enough to take me into your confidence.'

'I took certain precautions for your safety,' he said defensively.

'Oh, yes. You had me followed, right? But you neglected to tell me about that either.' She paused and thrust her hands into the deep pockets of her robe. 'You know, I haven't been sleeping and I've lost weight. I've been looking over my shoulder for weeks, jumping every time the phone rings, imagining all kinds of horrors. If I had just known that you were there, in the background . . . Didn't it occur to you that I'd be affected by all this? Maybe that didn't matter.

You just can't unbend, can you? You're so sure that you can handle everything by yourself, never mind who gets hurt in the process.'

'Marika, please. That's not true—'

'It is true, Stone. You give just so much and then you call a halt. There's a streak of coldness in you, a remoteness, that pushes people away. You don't trust anyone and you don't give anything of yourself – at least, not beyond the physical. You'll end up old and alone, if you carry on this way. Is that what you want?'

She saw that he had gone pale, but she was too far gone to hold back now. This was the pay-off for all that she had endured. She wanted to hurt him, to shock him into a single honest reaction.

'The Major distrusts you too,' she said. 'He doesn't know what to think. He's old and ill. The last thing he needs is this. Surely you owe him an explanation.'

Stone's face was set and his dark eyes were shadowed by fury. Marika sensed that she had ventured into forbidden territory.

'Don't bring the Major into this,' Stone said. 'You're as bad as he is! You speak of trust. Well it works both ways, you know. Why didn't he give me the benefit of the doubt? Why didn't you? You claim to know me so well. I thought that I was acting in good faith. All right, maybe I ought to have confided in you, but I believed that I was protecting you by keeping information to myself. It would have been so easy for you to slip up and warn Charles, inadvertently maybe, but it was a possibility I had to take into account. You know now what he's capable of. Think what he might have done to you.'

He stretched out a hand.

'Come and sit here. Don't you think that Charles would just love this? You and me at each other's throats? It's as if he's still exerting some influence over us.'

As Marika absorbed the truth of his words she felt her anger fading. Stone was right. In a way it was as if Charles had won after all. And that could not be. She sank down onto the sofa.

'All right. I concede that you acted for the best, as you saw it. It's all over now and no real harm's been done. But you've hurt me badly, Stone, and I wanted you to know that. I'm not going to keep pretending that it's OK for us to just have sex and play erotic power games. There's more to us than that. I know it and you do too. And I really don't care whether you choose to admit to that or not.'

She leaned against the sofa back, her eyes closed. It had been a long, gruelling day. Her foot was throbbing again and all she wanted to do was go to sleep. The silence stretched between them, vibrating with things unsaid.

I've burnt my bridges now, she thought, I've said the one thing guaranteed to make him take to his heels. A man who lived for pleasure, the thrill of the chase, and the erotic charge of being an active member of the Discipline of Pearls did not want to be reminded of responsibility or worse still, commitment.

But she was past caring. If he wanted to leave now, fine. She did not have to watch him go.

She felt the cushions move as Stone rose to his feet. In a moment he would cross the room to the front door. That would be about right, she thought, bitterly. He could face any amount of physical danger, but when it came to facing up to his feelings it was no go. Just like many men she knew, Stone was a moral coward.

He surprised her completely by laying gentle hands on her and pulling her to her feet.

'Come on. You're about finished. And no wonder, after what you've been through. I'm sorry, Marika. You're right. I should have trusted you. I know that now. It's not easy for me to open up. I've been taking care of number one for too long.'

She could hardly believe her ears. Stone, apologising. It was unheard of. Leaning against him as he helped her into the bedroom, she breathed in the smell of him. The night air was fresh on his hair and his familiar woody cologne only partly masked the scent of clean maleness.

She allowed him to take off her towelling robe and woollen socks. When he had folded back the bedclothes, she sank onto the bed and laid her head on the welcome softness of a pillow. Kneeling by the side of the bed, he leaned over to kiss her cheek.

'I knew that it was a mistake to become involved with you,' he said, smiling to soften his words. 'I never wanted to feel like this about any woman.'

She smiled sleepily.

'And I'm not looking for that one special man in my life. But things have a habit of creeping up on you, don't they?'

'Maybe,' he said, ruefully. 'But I won't deceive you. It's a mistake to expect too much of me. Be satisfied with what there is, Marika. That way, neither of us will get hurt.'

Her eyes drooped and she saw the movement of his hand as he put something on her bedside cabinet. It was the paper wallet containing the photographs and negatives.

'Thanks,' she whispered, then with a flash of her usual humour, said, 'I hope you enjoyed looking at them.'

Stone laughed.

'Very much,' he said. 'You're still my most accomplished protégée. I would have hated to lose you to Charles's degraded secret society. You're much too good for that.'

He was still chuckling as he left the room. She heard

the front door slam after him. It was an odd note to part on, but as she drifted into sleep she felt happier than she had for weeks.

For the first time Stone had actually admitted that he cared for her. And that was a landmark indeed.

It was almost a week later that the sound of the letterbox snapping shut reached Marika in the kitchen, where she was breakfasting on poached eggs, tomatoes, and toast.

She walked into the hall, nibbling a slice of buttered toast and picked up the letters lying on her mat. While she opened her post she finished eating her meal. Her appetite seemed to have returned with a vengeance, now that she was free of the spectre of Charles.

It was only now that she realised just how much she had been affected by his campaign to bully and frighten her into submitting to him. She was sleeping well and waking refreshed and eager to face whatever the day held. The lines of worry and other signs of strain around her mouth had disappeared overnight.

Most of the post consisted of bills. There was also a bank statement and a postcard from Pia. It appeared that the model was on location in the Australian outback, filming an advertisement for a famous brand of lager.

Pia's card was full of complaints about the heat, the dust, and the animal life.

'Even the worms here have teeth,' she had written. 'I can't wait to be home in good old grey damp Britain.'

Marika smiled, thinking of the time they had spent in Rome. Pia occupied a special place in her thoughts and in her life, as did Rafael, but she was honest enough to admit that no one, but no one, affected her the way that Stone did.

She sighed, wondering if they would ever resolve

their differences. He had not been in touch since the night Charles was arrested.

'What have we here?' she said aloud as she opened an envelope with a handwritten address and a London postmark.

The black card, plain except for a telephone number in raised gold lettering, fell on to the kitchen table. Marika picked it up and ran her thumb over the numbers.

Her pulses quickened. There was only one person who could have sent such a card, one person who had the audacity to summon her as if she was a rookie, freshly recruited to the society. Without hesitation, she dialled the number on the card.

'Hello, Marika,' said Stone. 'I'm glad that you called me so promptly.'

'I was curious,' she said. 'No one has sent me a black card for a while.'

'Ah, no doubt you think you have risen above such things. None of us in the Discipline of Pearls should forget how we started. The rituals of giving and demanding pleasure, of putting oneself into the trust of a master or mistress are good for us. They stop us becoming too self-important, don't you think?'

Despite his light, conversational tone, Marika felt a shiver of excitement. This was how it was to be then. Perhaps it was time to face up to the fact that Stone would never step out of the persona he was most comfortable with.

If she wanted him, then it must be within the terms laid down by the Discipline of Pearls. A love affair within a ritual. It was an intriguing prospect.

'So, this is to be a lesson – for me?' she said coolly. 'On this assignment, who is to be the giver of pleasure and who is the receiver?'

He laughed huskily.

'That, as ever, is not a simple thing to answer. The

192

edges have become blurred between you and me, have they not? Perhaps that's why I find you so exciting. Now. No more talk. We ought at least try to keep to the rules. Have you a pen and paper? Good. Then take this down . . .'

Chapter Thirteen

WITH THE NOTEPAD containing Stone's instructions in her hand, Marika phoned Gwen.

'I have to leave for Austria around lunchtime,' she said. 'I'm afraid it was a last minute arrangement. Something I didn't anticipate. I expect to be gone for a few days. Will you cope?'

'Don't I always?' Gwen said jauntily. 'No problem. You go off and net this new client or whatever you have to do. Can I ask you one thing?'

'What's that?'

'Is this trip going to put the roses back in your cheeks? I've been pretty worried about you lately. You're less tense, but you're still not yourself.'

Marika smiled. This kind of comment was the nearest Gwen ever got to prying into her private life. She felt a rush of affection for the older woman.

'Oh, I think you can count on me making a full recovery,' she said. 'Thanks for your concern. I'll phone you when I get to my hotel and leave you a contact number for emergencies.'

'Fine,' Gwen said, and Marika could tell that she was grinning. 'But it seems to me that the emergency's over. Have fun. You deserve it. See you in a while.'

Marika put the phone down and began taking

hangers out of her wardrobe.

Stone had told her to bring an evening dress. She chose one she had bought for a gala evening and worn only once before. It was an elegant Versace, a classic in panelled black velvet. After selecting jewellery and underwear to go with the dress, she grabbed other garments almost at random, folding them hurriedly into her weekend case. Finally, having finished packing, she dressed for the journey in loose trousers and an over-sized top in an uncrushable, teal blue fabric.

Two hours later she was on the plane and leaving Heathrow. The flight to Austria was smooth and trouble free and there were no hold-ups at the airport. She read a crime paperback for a while and then sat looking out of the plane window, captivated by the colours of a sunset which were reflected off a bank of clouds; orange, magenta, violet.

The now familiar feeling of excitement settled in the pit of her stomach. She cast her mind back over all the meetings with Stone. Each of the times they had shared an encounter, it had been challenging or shocking; stretching her to the limits of imagination and sexual endurance. What else could there be for her to experience at his hands?

The connection for Vienna was on schedule. Marika slept for much of the second part of the journey and arrived at the terminal feeling fresh and rested. The evening air was thin and cool and held the tang of pine resin. Delicious. Marika drew it into her lungs as she walked the few yards towards the waiting taxi. She gave the driver directions, then sat back to enjoy the scenery.

Against the backdrop of a sky coloured greyish-purple, the snow-capped mountains looked beautiful and mysterious. Forests of fir trees clothed the lower slopes and swept down to the glassy surface of a picture-book lake. There was a stillness about everything that was majestic.

By the time the taxi slid to a halt in front of the hotel, the sky had darkened and was alight with the silver points of stars.

The hotel was a three-storey building, built on a slope overlooking Lake Constance. It had colourful painted balconies and walls clad with traditionally-worked wooden panels. Marika was shown to a room on the top floor, with a view over the lake. From her window she could see the lights strung out along the shore. There were many tourists in evidence, no doubt attracted to Vienna for the concerts.

The beacons of the many anchored boats were reflected in the dark waters, giving a festive ambience to the area. Charmed by her first sight of Vienna, Marika opened the window and the lilting strains of a Strauss waltz floated into her room.

'How beautiful,' she breathed.

It seemed an unlikely setting for a meeting with Stone. She wondered if he had checked to see if she had arrived at the hotel. So far he had not contacted her. She would have to wait for him to make his move. His last instruction had been for her to dress for the opera.

After unpacking, she showered and changed into clean underwear. Using a hot brush she curled her hair, then pinned it high and arranged it into elegant loops. The style suited her, showing off her slim neck and jawline. She applied make-up, darkening her eyes dramatically and applying a pillar-box red lipstick to her mouth.

The reflection in the wardrobe mirror showed a poised young woman, her waist cinched in by a black satin corset and the tops of her breasts bulging provocatively upwards.

Marika smoothed her hands over her waist, then

196

stroked the rich swell of her hips. A tiny triangle of cobweb-fine, black lace covered her pubis and her legs were encased in sheeny black stockings. High-heeled shoes of black satin, trimmed with tiny diamanté buckles, flattered her calves and ankles.

She smiled, knowing that she had never looked better. Whatever Stone had planned, he would not be disappointed by her appearance.

She was battling with the zip of the slim-fitting evening dress, when there was a knock at the door. Thinking that it would be a bell boy with a message, she hurried to open it. It was a complete surprise to find Stone standing there.

'Oh, I . . . didn't expect you,' she faltered. 'I'm not quite ready. Come in. Please.'

She was annoyed to find that she felt flustered. In a few more minutes she would have been groomed to within an inch of her life and ready for whatever grand entrance he had planned.

Stone's early arrival had thrown her off balance. She knew that her reaction was merely fleeting. This was the old Marika speaking, the Marika who had planned her life down to the last detail and who loved order in all things.

She had come a long way since those days.

'You seem disappointed,' Stone said dryly. 'Perhaps you would have preferred a cryptic note instead of a personal appearance?'

'Disappointed? Never that,' she said.

God, he looked fantastic in a formal dark suit and white shirt. His dark hair hung in glossy strands to his shoulders. She realised that he was teasing her and smiled.

'You chose your moment perfectly. I need some help. Would you mind? I can't seem to fasten this zip right up to the top.'

His fingers were warm as they brushed against her

nape. For an instant he pressed his lips to the side of her neck and she closed her eyes with pleasure.

'There,' he said. 'Finished. Ready now?'

'Just a moment. My earrings.'

Her fingers were trembling as she affixed the diamanté drop-style earrings. How strange, she thought, even after everything that's happened, after working my way up through the ranks of the Discipline of Pearls, I feel like some gauche schoolgirl in Stone's presence.

It was a disquieting, but exciting sensation. Whatever Stone was, he was not a man she could take for granted.

'Time to leave. We have a boat to catch,' Stone said, taking hold of her arm and leading her towards the door.

'But . . . my coat.'

'You won't need it. We have to leave at once.'

She found herself obeying meekly. Stone might have come to collect her in person, acting the part of the polite escort, but he was plainly taking the upper hand now.

She glanced up at him once and found that his dark brooding eyes were sweeping over her from head to toe. The heat curdled in her veins.

'Do you approve of my appearance?' she said, lightly, unable to resist teasing him just a little. 'I dressed as you asked me to.'

The panelled black velvet dress with its deep collar was reminiscent of a fifties ballgown. Worn off the shoulder, the neckline was stunning. It fitted her perfectly and she knew that she had never looked better. She felt like Audrey Hepburn and Marilyn Monroe rolled into one, her creamy skin and blonde hair a perfect foil for the denseness of the black fabric.

Stone nodded curtly. 'You'll pass. Now, no more talk. Come with me.'

His face was impassive, but his eyes glittered with humour and approval. Like Marika, he was perfectly aware of the roles they were playing. All emotion, humour, passion, everything that was unsaid between them was transmuted into the ritual of their erotic encounter.

The ritual of pearls.

This sexual game-play, the pursuit of pleasure, which took them both out of the ordinary run of life, was perhaps the only place where she would ever meet Stone on equal terms. And while part of her still fought against the limits he imposed on their relationship, part of her could appreciate that there was a sort of poetry in accepting these restrictions.

I choose to give him mastery of my body on this occasion, she thought, I love how it feels when I allow him to propel me towards new pathways of pleasure.

Her knees felt weak as they left the hotel and walked the few yards to a landing stage, where a pleasure cruiser waiting to transport guests to the nearby opera house was moored. Men and women in evening dress were boarding the vessel and Stone and Marika took their place in the line. Moonlight glinted off richly coloured satins and silks and struck sparks from the array of jewellery.

Marika and Stone boarded the cruiser. He led the way. Plush leather seats were ranged along the sides of the cruiser, giving the passengers an unobstructed view of the lake, but Stone steered Marika past these.

Near the back of the cruiser there was a small cabin, separated from the public area by a wooden screen with a large window set into it. Stone ducked his head to negotiate the low doorway and Marika followed him. Upholstered seats of white leather were arranged around a curved window to form a narrow couch.

There was an ice-bucket, with a bottle of champagne, on a low table of pale wood. The same wood lined the walls. The tiny cabin was comfortable and had an air of intimacy, but it was hardly private. Marika's heart gave a lurch, beginning to suspect that this lack of privacy was the reason why Stone had chosen to bring her to this place.

Stone sat on one of the curved seats. Marika assumed that she was to do the same, but he held up his hand.

'Ah, no. Don't sit down. Take off your dress.'

Marika hesitated.

'Now? But the passengers are still coming on board.'

'Exactly,' he said evenly.

She glanced into the body of the cruiser. Many of the late boarders would have to pass by the small cabin and she would be visible through the screen window. Stone appeared to understand the reason for her consternation, but was unmoved by it. She could see that he was excited by the prospect of making love to her within sight and sound of the other passengers.

'I'm waiting,' he said huskily, moving his hand down to cup the bulge at his groin. 'And I'm ready.'

Marika's lips curved. This was a dare, a test to see how far she would go. Right. She would call his bluff.

Slowly, keeping her eyes on his hand which was stroking and moulding the thick column of his cock, she reached behind her and unzipped the dress. It was easier than she expected, since Stone had not fastened the topmost hook and eye back at the hotel room.

The velvet dress slid down her body and pooled on the floor. She was gratified by the flare of heat in Stone's eyes when he saw the corset, which covered her from breast to hip. The boned garment gave her an almost hour-glass figure. Lifting her chin she gave him a challenging look and put her hands on her hips.

'You look superb,' Stone said, beckoning to her to come closer.

She kept her eyes on his face as she approached him. The smell of him intoxicated her.

'Suck me,' he ordered, not bothering to lower his voice.

Marika's eyes opened wide with shock. The most she had expected was a brief, exciting coupling in a corner of the cabin, with both of them muffling their sighs of pleasure. But Stone wanted her to fellate him and it seemed not to matter to him that people might see her doing so.

The prospect thrilled and appalled her in equal measure. Why not? She dared not glance over her shoulder for fear that she would see someone looking into the cabin, but neither could she disobey Stone.

That was the unspoken rule of the society. Once the roles were established, they must be strictly adhered to.

Shielding Stone's hips and limbs with her own body, she knelt before him. Reaching out, she unzipped his fly and reached into the gap in his trousers. He made no move to help but looked down at her, a sardonic curve to his lips.

Yes, I know that it's risky, he seemed to be saying, that's why it's so exciting. Marika's blood pounded. She had to agree.

Closing her hand around his hot flesh she drew his cock free. The reddened shaft twitched as she closed her lips around the glans. He tasted faintly of salt and something richer, almost animal. With slack lips she pleasured the swollen bulb, before moving down the stem, flicking out her tongue to tease him with little licks.

Stone arched his back and cupped the back of her head with his hand. Opening his fly wider, she continued on down to the firm sac of his balls and licked them gently, feeling the fine hairs that grew there tickling her tongue. Stone moaned softly under his breath as she worked her way back up his cock, sucking more strongly and lapping the sensitive place on the underside of his glans.

201

'Enough,' he grunted, pushing her away. 'Bring me the champagne.'

The abrupt change of tempo threw her for a moment, but she moved to do as he asked. The bottle was ice-cold against her hand and it was a relief when he took it from her.

'Get up on to the seat,' he said. 'Lie back and spread your legs.'

Slowly Marika did so. She was facing the window that gave onto the interior of the cruiser now and she prayed that no one would glance their way.

Stone reached out and trailed a finger across her lace-covered mound. The division of her labia was clearly visible through the fine fabric and he caressed her lingeringly, running the tip of a nail over her closed slit and pressing on the place which hid her throbbing bud.

Marika's thighs flexed, tremors passing over the creamy flesh at the subtle, scratchy pressure against her clitoris. Slipping two fingers under the flimsy side-straps of her panties, Stone eased them down. For a moment they were stretched tautly between her parted thighs, like a bridge, then he pulled them free and tossed them on the floor.

The heat rose into Marika's face as he took hold of her sex, pressing the swollen lips open almost roughly and gazing down at her rosy flesh. She expected him to mount her and knew by his expression that he was considering doing just that, but he ran his thumbs over her labia once or twice and then sat back.

Marika almost squirmed with impatience as Stone turned his attention to her breasts. Sliding his hands up her body, he reached under the boned front of the corset and lifted her breasts free. They lolled slightly to either side of her chest, pushed into prominent, pear-shaped mounds by the garment which still constricted her waist.

'I love your nipples. Make them hard for me,' he said.

While Marika pinched and rolled, working the little knots of flesh into hard, red-brown buttons, Stone began twisting the metal that held the champagne cork in place. Marika watched him. He looked so cool and calm, while she was almost aching with embarrassment, acutely aware of how exposed she was.

My God, we could be arrested for indecency, she thought.

Then she gasped aloud and ceased to think at all. The champagne cork popped, with a sound like a cannon going off, and a freezing wave of champagne fizzed over her lower belly and spread open sex. The gush of coldness against her throbbing membranes only served to arouse her even more.

There were sounds of laughter and clapping from the passengers and she blushed hotly, expecting at any moment to see faces pressed against the window.

Nothing of the sort happened and she gave a sigh of relief mixed with pleasure as Stone began lapping champagne from her belly and inner thighs. She tensed, longing for him to bring his mouth to her groin, arching her back to encourage him towards more intimate caresses. Oh God, she was dying for the feel of his tongue.

In a moment he drew back and she saw that he had the champagne cork in his hand. Bringing it to his mouth he closed his lips around it, wetting it with saliva. Marika's vagina pulsed with eagerness. He was going to push it into her, she just knew it. How depraved she would look, with the cork sticking out of her body, the swollen rim of it preventing it from going right into her. The prospect was unbearably exciting.

'Oh, yes . . .' she breathed, opening her legs as wide as possible and lifting her hips.

At that moment she felt completely female. There

was something almost timeless about offering up the moist, red mouth of her vagina to him. It was as if she was some ancient priestess engaged in a sacred rite. She wanted to be filled, penetrated. It was awful to accept the fact that she was eager for his every touch, prepared to do almost anything in the pursuit of their shared pleasures.

But she wasn't prepared for his next words.

'Turn over and get up on all fours.'

She trembled as she realised what he meant to do and the desire within her warred with the shame. It was not her vagina he wished to penetrate. The imminent act had always been difficult for her. It was the final taboo and she could not help shying away from him, her buttocks tightening involuntarily.

Stone ordered her to put her head down and lift her bottom into the air. She did so slowly, knowing that nothing was hidden from him. The delicate, inner surfaces of her cheeks, her creased anus, and the ripe fruit of her sex were all on view to him; presented ready for whatever he planned to do.

Her face burned at Stone's next words.

'Hold yourself open. You know what I want from you.'

Reaching around slowly, she exerted pressure on her bottom feeling the tight nether orifice gape open a little. She bit her lip as Stone stroked her anus with a wet finger, working the tip inside her a little way until the ring of muscle relaxed.

Then she felt the cork pressing into her. It was cold initially and Marika's flesh twitched at the first touch of it on her skin. Stone worked it into her slowly, giving her time to get used to the sensation of being stretched.

As he worked the cork in and out of the tight hole, he put one hand between her legs and pinched and rubbed her swollen button. The tears squeezed from

204

between Marika's lids. They were not tears of pain, since her body accommodated the object with little difficulty. The reasons she wept were complex; she did not understand why herself, save that she felt so vulnerable, so wonderfully *used*, and, in the strangest way, free to enjoy a pleasure she would not have sought for herself.

Gasping and bucking against his hand she climaxed. Stone stroked her buttocks and inner thighs, murmuring all the time, 'I know that this is a difficult pleasure for you. That's why I insist on it. I want everything you have at this moment. Your obedience, your pleasure, your shame.'

And my love, she thought, you want that too. Though you dare not say it. But wasn't what they were doing a form of love?

She gave a groan of need, her climax having taken only the edge from her desire for Stone, and felt the cork move within her. Stone's fingers were still on her sex, smoothing open her wet labia he tapped gently on the hard bead of her clitoris. In a moment she was going to come again. She could hardly hold back the tide of sensations.

'Please. Do it to me,' she groaned.

Stone pulled her to the edge of the seat and she felt the blunt head of his cock enter her. He slid straight into her, right into the heart of her silken darkness. She bit back a scream as the incredible pleasure gripped her belly. Never had she felt so filled, so wonderfully used. The cork in her bottom felt like a second penis as it moved in time with Stone's thrusts.

Marika forgot where she was. It did not matter that they would attract attention. She moaned aloud, mashing her bottom against Stone's flat belly, wanting the feelings to go on and on. Just when she felt the ripples of another orgasm begin, Stone gripped her head and twisted her round to the side so that she was

205

forced to look towards the window.

A ring of faces were pressed to the glass. Perhaps they had been watching for some time. Marika no longer cared. Chewing at her bottom lip, her hips weaving and thrashing, she dissolved into a mind-blowing climax. Stone came almost immediately, his cock lodged deeply inside her, the force of his flat belly pushing the anal plug in as far as it would go.

For a moment neither of them could move, then, with the release of her sexual tension, Marika saw the funny side of the situation.

'Perhaps we should send a hat round for donations,' she said, beginning to giggle, softly at first, then to laugh aloud.

Stone laughed too, a deep bass chuckle, as he removed the cork. He bent over to place a kiss on each of her buttocks before he stood up and passed her her panties.

'There's really no hope for you as a sex slave, you know,' he joked. 'I don't know what I see in you.'

'Must be my addictive personality,' she said.

It was good to laugh with him. Somehow they had achieved something she would never have dreamed possible. Real friendship and mutual liking. Perhaps that was rarer than passion.

As Marika dressed, she smiled tremulously at the passengers. There was a burst of applause from them.

'Bravo!'

They called out, waving and applauding.

'A virtuoso performance! Bravo!'

In a while the watchers dispersed and went back to their seats. Dressed again and hardly looking ruffled, Marika sipped the glass of champagne which Stone passed her. A suspicion had been forming for some time and she lifted a questioning brow.

'Hadn't you better come clean?'

He grinned wickedly.

'All right. I suppose I'd better own up. This isn't a public craft, as I led you to believe. The passengers are singularly important guests and we're on our way to a singularly important meeting.'

Suddenly Marika knew that it had something to do with the Discipline of Pearls. She said so to Stone. He nodded.

'Very astute of you. I thought it was about time I made my peace with the Major. Your comments about him really made me think. He's convalescing in this area and the wily old devil has taken the opportunity to call a grand meeting of the society. Just like him not to miss a trick. Also a celebration seemed in order. Charles Germain is no longer a threat to any of us. I wonder if you realise just how powerful that man was. No matter. That's all over now. It's widely believed that you are due for promotion for your part in helping to bring about Charles's downfall.'

'But I did nothing, except make a mess of things. It was all due to you—'

Stone put two fingers to her lips.

'No arguments please. I couldn't have nailed the bastard without you. You'll have to accept this version of a public apology. It's the best you'll ever get. Right?'

'Right,' she said.

'Now. We're almost at our destination. The Major is waiting for us and, so I believe, are a number of other people you know.'

Marika was hardly able to encompass the turn of events. For the first time she was actually going to meet the cream of the Discipline of Pearls. She was conscious of the importance of this meeting. It meant that she was one of the elite, but she did not know what that would mean in the future.

The one thing she did know, was that she and Stone were going to the meeting as a couple. It was a public declaration of their mutual involvement within the society.

And that had to mean that there was hope for the future.

Didn't it?

WARNING: These titles are *X Rated* . . .

PRIVATE ACT
Zara Devereux

> *'She was completely powerless under Gerard's domination, with no responsibility, no say in what was done to her. He tied her wrists together with a scarf and secured them to the legs of the stool, then set about tethering her ankles . . .'*

Kasia Lyndon is a good-looking but struggling young actress who is thrilled to get her first break at the Craven Playhouse, a privately owned theatre company in a country manor house.

But this is no ordinary theatre, and she must live her role both on and off stage – even when it demands that she submits herself to her sadistic leading man and his mistress. Kasia, however, soon discovers that this domination has unleashed feelings in her that she never dreamt she had.

THE DOMINATRIX
Emma Allan

'Karen looked in the mirror again. She hardly recognised herself. The tight basque, the stockings and the high-heeled shoes had transformed her body. Her breasts looked yielding and impossibly creamy in contrast to the shiny red satin. She looked like an expensive whore . . .'

Karen Masters has never been very interested in sex. But when she sees a video of her friend Barbara engaging in some very *outré* sex games with her husband Dan, she begins to realise what she has been missing.

Beautiful redhead Pamela Stern is a dominatrix and more than willing to show Karen exactly what this means. As she wields the whip Karen's sexuality comes alive, and when she discovers that one of Pamela's clients is her own boss Malcolm Travers, she agrees to become his personal dominatrix. Now Karen can fully explore the limits of her own desires, at least until Malcolm's wife finds out . . .

SECRET FANTASY
Vanessa Davies

'Stella noticed the fur-lined handcuffs that Katya had left hanging on the back of a chair. Maybe it was time she took the challenge of Mark herself! A warm, intoxicating thrill spread through her body, but it wasn't just sexual. She recognised its primal nature immediately: it was the thrill of the chase!'

Stella and Katya hold sexy parties in a Surrey mansion, where perverse desires are satisfied in a fetish room called the O-Zone. When mysterious Mark turns up, Stella is baffled by his cool indifference to the raunchy goings-on around him.

Both women try to discover his private fantasies, but only Stella comes close. When Katya discovers her secret diary, their rivalry over Mark threatens to drive the women apart . . .

HOUSE OF DECADENCE
Lucia Cubelli

'"Why do you keep tormenting me?" she moaned, as his hand left her breasts and crept down between her spread thighs.

"Because I love watching you struggle as you learn each lesson," explained Fabrizio. "I want to teach you everything there is to know about sex. I promised you that your life would change if you came here, and I always keep my promises."'

At 23, Megan Stewart feels there should be more to life than working in a public library so she answers an advert for a post in a country house – and discovers what she has been missing.

Handsome Fabrizio Balocchi is far from his Tuscan home and feeling bored. But he instinctively knows that Megan will be a natural player in his games of domination and, step by step, he leads her into a darker world, a world where pleasure is mixed with pain. Now Megan must decide how far she is willing to go in order to stay in Fabrizio's house of decadence . . .

The Ritual of Pearls

THE X LIBRIS READERS SURVEY

We hope you will take a moment to fill out this questionnaire and tell us more about what you want to read – and how we can provide it!

1. About you ...

A)   Male   Female

B)   Under 21   41–50
            21–30   51–60
            31–40   Over 60

C)   Occupation_____

D)   Annual household income:
            under £10,000   £31–40,000
            £11–20,000   £41–50,000
            £21–30,000   Over £50,000

E)   At what age did you leave full-time education?

            16 or younger   20 or older
            17–19   still in education

2. About X Libris ...

A)   How did you acquire this book?

       I bought it myself
       I borrowed/found it
       Someone else bought it for me

B)   How did you find out about X Libris books?

       In a shop
       In a magazine
       Other_____

C)   Please tick any statements you agree with:

       I would feel more comfortable about buying X Libris books if the covers were less explicit

       I wish the covers of X Libris books were more explicit

       I think X Libris covers are just right

       If you could design your own X Libris cover, how would it look?

D)   Do you read X Libris books in public places (for example, on trains, at bus stops, etc.)?

       Yes   No

3. About this book ...

A) Do you think this book has:

Too much sex?
Not enough?
It's about right?

B) Do you think the writing in this book is:

Too unreal/escapist?
Too everyday?
About right?

C) Do you find the story in this book:

Too complicated?
Too boring/simple?
About right?

D) How many X Libris books have you read?

If you have a favourite X Libris book, what is its title?

Why do you like it so much?

4. Your ideal X Libris book ...

A) Using a scale from 1 (lowest) to 5 (highest), please rate the following possible settings for an X Libris book:

Roman/Medieval/Barbarian
Elizabethan/Renaissance/Restoration
Victorian/Edwardian
The Jazz Age (1920s & 30s)
Present day
Future
Other

B) Using the same scale of 1 to 5, please rate the following sexual possibilities for an X Libris book:

Submissive male/dominant female
Submissive female/dominant male
Lesbian sex
Gay male sex
Bondage/fetishism
Romantic love
Experimental sex (for example, anal/watersports/sex toys)
Group sex

C) Using the same scale of 1 to 5, please rate the following writing styles you might find in an X Libris book:

Realistic, down to earth, a true-to-life situation
Fantasy, escapist, but just possible
Completely unreal, out of bounds, dreamlike

D) From whose viewpoint would you prefer your ideal X Libris book to be written?

Main male characters
Main female characters
Both

E) What would your ideal X Libris heroine be like?

Dominant	Shy
Extroverted	Glamorous
Independent	Bisexual
Adventurous	Naïve
Intellectual	Kinky
Professional	Introverted
Successful	Ordinary
Other	

F) What would your ideal X Libris hero be like?

Caring	Athletic
Cruel	Sophisticated
Debonair	Retiring
Naïve	Outdoors type
Intellectual	Rugged
Professional	Kinky
Romantic	Hunky
Successful	Effeminate
Ordinary	Executive type
Sexually dominant	Sexually submissive
Other	

G) Is there one particular setting or subject matter that your ideal X Libris book would contain?

H) Please feel free to tell us about anything else you like/dislike about X Libris if we haven't asked you.

Thank you for taking time to tell us what you think about X Libris. Please tear this questionnaire out of the book now and post it back to us:

X Libris
Brettenham House
Lancaster Place
London WC2E 7EN

Other bestselling X Libris titles available by mail: